Kevin said.

Michelle pulled her arm free. "No. I don't need a doctor. I just want to go home and go to bed."

Kevin grabbed her arm and pulled her in the opposite direction. "Michelle, we can argue later. Something's wrong...."

She broke free. "Kevin, please..." She clamped her hand over her mouth. "I know what's wrong and you can't help. Just let me by."

His dark, determined eyes looked by turns worried and suspicious. "What do you mean? What's wrong with you?"

This wasn't the time, or the place. But she had to get past him. *Now!* "I'm pregnant, and I'm going to throw up all over you if you don't move this instant."

Before he could respond, she rushed out of the room....

Dear Reader,

Established stars and exciting new names...that's what's in store for you this month from Silhouette Desire. Let's begin with Cait London's MAN OF THE MONTH, *Tallchief's Bride*—it's also the latest in her wonderful series, THE TALLCHIEFS.

The fun continues with *Babies by the Busload*, the next book in Raye Morgan's THE BABY SHOWER series, and *Michael's Baby*, the first installment of Cathie Linz's delightful series, THREE WEDDINGS AND A GIFT.

So many of you have indicated how much you love the work of Peggy Moreland, so I know you'll all be excited about her latest sensuous romp, *A Willful Marriage*. And Anne Eames, who made her debut earlier in the year in Silhouette Desire's Celebration 1000, gives us more pleasure with *You're What?!* And if you enjoy a little melodrama with your romance, take a peek at Metsy Hingle's enthralling new book, *Backfire*.

As always, each and every Silhouette Desire is sensuous, emotional and sure to leave you feeling good at the end of the day!

Happy Reading!

*Lucia Macro*

Senior Editor

Please address questions and book requests to:
Silhouette Reader Service
U.S.: 3010 Walden Ave., P.O. Box 1325, Buffalo, NY 14269
Canadian: P.O. Box 609, Fort Erie, Ont. L2A 5X3

# ANNE EAMES
## YOU'RE WHAT?!

SILHOUETTE *Desire*

Published by Silhouette Books

America's Publisher of Contemporary Romance

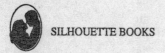

SILHOUETTE BOOKS

ISBN 0-373-76025-6

YOU'RE WHAT?!

**Books by Anne Eames**

Silhouette Desire

*Two Weddings and a Bride* #996
*You're What?!* #1025

---

## ANNE EAMES

has a varied background, including managing a theater, a bridal salon and a construction association, netting several marketing and communication awards along the way. In 1991 she joined the Romance Writers of America, later becoming a Golden Heart finalist, the winner of the Maggie Award, and finally a published author—her lifelong dream.

Anne and her engineer husband, Bill, live in southeastern Michigan and share a family of five—two hers (Tim and Tom), two his (Erin and David) and one theirs (an adorable miniature dachshund, Punkin).

To "S" for planting this "seed"
to Lisa and Linda for their medical contributions
to Billie and Ellen for their cruise stories
and especially
to my own private hero...Bill

# One

"Sperm bank!" Michelle groused aloud and shook her head in disbelief. "Who would've thought it would come to this?"

She rolled her eyes and slouched on the edge of the examining table. With a paper sheet tucked tightly under her arms, she scraped nonexistent dirt from beneath her freshly manicured nails.

Thirty-six years old, divorced, and no man on the horizon. What choice did she have? She glanced at her watch for the umpteenth time. It's not as though she hadn't given the system a chance. In the three years since she'd been back on the single scene, she'd had her share of dates—enough to make her more than a little cynical about finding Mr. Right. Besides, the longer she was on her own, the more she liked it.

She heard a door open and close in the next room. Michelle stopped playing with her fingers and dropped them in her lap. This anxiety was counterproductive. She had to control her wavering emotions and think positive thoughts.

For a start, she remembered this morning's clear blue sky and the weatherman's prediction of sixty-two degrees by noon—

almost unheard-of for mid-March in Detroit. If being here was
wrong, surely there'd be a blizzard with icy, impassable roads.
The paper crinkled under her legs as she shifted positions and
wrestled with her nagging doubts.

Looking for a distraction, she surveyed the small, sterile
room. White walls displayed framed photographs of pudgy-
cheeked cherubs, each one seeming to smile in her direction,
each tweaking her heartstrings and causing her eyes to mist
over. More than anything, she wanted a baby. If only there was
another way...

After a loud knock, the door flew open beside her. Startled,
she twisted toward it. An intense, white-coated doctor sprang
into the room, his entrance instantly reminding her of Kramer
on the sitcom "Seinfeld." She almost laughed before eyeing the
footlong sheathed instrument in his hand.

Ceremoniously, the doctor placed the syringelike object on
a stainless-steel tray, then picked up her chart and perused his
notes. Michelle studied his thick crop of wildly curly hair until
he lifted his gaze. Finally, he flashed a wide smile, exposing
large white teeth.

"Michelle Purdue! And how are you?"

Great! Another poet. She hated it when anyone rhymed her
name in that singsong way. "Fine... I guess."

An exaggerated frown replaced his smile. Deep furrows
creased his high forehead. "You guess? Oh-oh. Second
thoughts?"

More like third, fourth or fifth. She lifted her chin and lied.
"No. Not at all." This was one strange man. But then what
kind of doctor would make a career at a place like this?

He put the chart down and rubbed his hands together, the
smile back on his long, angular face. "Good. Then today's the
day. Right?"

She smiled back and nodded. "Right." He was almost vi-
brating with energy. She hoped it was his eccentric personality,
or too much coffee. The alternatives were scary.

"Any questions?"

She thought about asking him if he'd ever watched "Seinfeld," but then she shook her head.

He grabbed the door handle with the same gusto as when he'd entered and called over his shoulder, "The nurse will be right in to get you ready."

Michelle let out a soft laugh as he exited but cut it short when a more sedate, middle-aged woman walked in behind him and closed the door.

"My name's Ellen. If there's anything I can do to make you more comfortable, just ask," she said, wasting no time in positioning each of Michelle's feet in cold, stainless-steel stirrups. This wasn't exactly making her feel more comfortable.

She squirmed on the hard table, knees pointing east and west. When her teeth began chattering and goose bumps appeared on her arms, she asked, "Is there anything warmer than this paper sheet?"

"Sure there is!" Ellen smiled sweetly. "I'll be right back."

Michelle drew her knees together in an attempt to retain some body heat and restore a modicum of dignity. But Ellen was back in seconds, covering her with a blanket and prying her legs apart once again.

Now the gray-haired nurse held up earphones in one hand and a half-dozen cassettes in the other. "Would you like to listen to a tape?" Michelle studied the selection and pointed to an instrumental medley of Andrew Lloyd Webber show tunes. Ellen inserted the tape and handed Michelle the headset.

"Anything else I can do for you, dear?"

How about bringing in Kevin Costner and dimming the lights? "A magazine would be nice," she said instead.

Ellen moved to a small wall-mounted rack. "*Good Housekeeping, Better Homes and Gardens* or *People?*" she asked.

Ah, the double standard. How successful would this place be if donors were given the same choice? "*People* will be fine, thank you."

Ellen moved toward what looked like a doorbell and pressed it. "The doctor will be back any moment." The nurse returned to the table and laid a warm hand on Michelle's shoulder. "Try to relax, dear. It will increase your chances of success, you know." Michelle glanced at the long tube on the tray and shuddered involuntarily. "I know it looks scary, but I'm sure Dr. Adam explained. It has to be that long in order to reach through the cervix and up to the eggs. There'll be some cramping, but not for long." With one last pat, she smiled and moved to her observation post at the end of the table.

Michelle closed her eyes and played with the volume on the headphones. She let her mind float with "The Music of the Night," for the moment ignoring the magazine on her chest. She wondered if she could relax enough to fall asleep. She had twenty minutes to lie here once the procedure was finished.

But before long, she felt Dr. Adam's latex-covered hands lift the covers, and she knew sleep was out of the question.

Heart pounding, she kept her eyes shut and conjured up images of Costner, hoping he would provide a respite from this bizarre reality. Her mind raced through his many roles, stopping when she remembered *Dances With Wolves*. The scene in which he was reunited with his pregnant wife after a long separation came into focus. She pictured him jumping off his horse and running to meet her. They kissed and hugged each other wildly, dropping into the snow, rolling in ecstasy, oblivious to those around them.

The doctor warned her she was about to feel some pressure. Michelle felt a cold steel instrument followed by more pain than she'd anticipated. A small groan passed her lips. Within seconds she felt a tug at the end of the table and she glanced down. The doctor lifted her feet from the stirrups and brought her legs together on the extended table. Then he gave her what she guessed was a reassuring wink and a quick pat on the knee, before brusquely leaving the room, Ellen in tow.

Michelle stared at the closed door, dumbstruck by the speed and cold efficiency of it all. But then what had she expected? For the doctor to lie down on the table next to her and offer her a cigarette? She looked at the ceiling and blinked away an unexpected tear. If she was going to be a single parent, she had better get used to going it alone.

Determined to recapture her earlier fantasy, she picked up the forgotten magazine and flipped through the pages, hoping to find her favorite actor's handsome face. All she found was Billy Crystal and Jack Palance with a big cow.

Exasperated, she slapped the magazine shut against her chest and pressed the earphones to her head. "Kevin, Kevin..." She shook her head and exhaled a long, weary breath. "Where are you when I need you?"

"Kevin!"

Dr. Kevin Singleton stopped at the end of the hall and looked over his shoulder, annoyance pinching his forehead.

The chief of staff, Paul Westerfield, closed the distance between them. "Have a couple minutes?"

Kevin looked at his watch, already knowing the answer. "Not really, Paul. Got one in postop and another up in half an hour."

Paul placed a hand on Kevin's shoulder and nudged him back toward his office. "I'll be brief."

Kevin eyed his friend as they stepped inside the office. Paul closed the door behind them and motioned for Kevin to sit. Instead of taking the seat beside him as usual, Paul sat heavily behind his desk, sending a clear message.

"Since you're in a hurry, I'll get right to the point."

Kevin crossed his arms, ready to take his medicine. It was probably another resident complaint. Those poor delicate egos. Okay. He'd take the reprimand, promise to try harder, and be out of here in two minutes.

"I've been looking over your schedule." Paul held up a printout. There were numerous pencil markings and what looked like calculations in the margins. "Are you aware that you logged more hours than any other doctor on staff last year? And outoperated the next-closest by nearly twenty percent?"

Kevin shrugged. It didn't surprise him. So where was the problem?

"And that this year you're ahead of last on a per-week basis?" Paul dropped the paper and leaned back, the creaking of his worn leather chair the only sound for the next few moments.

Kevin watched and waited while Paul studied him over the rims of his half glasses. Finally Kevin propped his elbows on his knees and hunched forward. "What? Just tell me."

"You're pushing yourself too hard, my friend...and you've lost something along the way."

Kevin bristled. "Like what?"

"Your sense of humor, for one thing."

Kevin slapped his hands on his knees, then stood. "I'll try to get to a comedy club next week. If that's it, I have work to do." He turned and started to leave.

"Sit down." Paul raised his voice, bringing Kevin back around. "We're not finished." He pointed to the seat.

Kevin ground his teeth. With great restraint, he lowered himself into the chair, not masking his irritation.

In a quieter voice, Paul continued. "We've been friends a long time, guy. I have to tell you, you're headed for trouble." He shook his head and smiled. "All work and no play. When was the last time you got—"

Kevin narrowed his eyes and glared. "Is this personal or business? Because if it's personal—"

"See what I mean? No sense of humor. I was going to ask, before you so rudely interrupted, when was the last time you got eight hours' sleep? But if you'd care to share other information with me, feel free."

Kevin slouched back in his seat. "Okay. Guess I had that one coming." Maybe he was a little uptight lately. If all Paul wanted him to do was shave a few hours off his schedule, he'd see what he could do.

"I'm not going to sit here and say I know how you feel. If my marriage ended like yours..." Kevin looked at the floor between his knees and Paul changed tacks. "It's been nearly four years, Kev. I know you don't need the money. Hell, you give more away than most people make. And the new cardiac care wing you donated is fully operational now. You can't use that project as an excuse anymore."

"Okay, okay. I'll cut back."

Paul took off his glasses and rubbed the bridge of his nose. "I've never pulled rank on you, Kev, but this time's different. It'll take more than cutting back. I've scheduled you for two weeks' vacation, beginning April 15th."

Kevin's head snapped up. "I can't. I have surgeries booked—"

"Reschedule."

"It's not that easy, I—"

"It never is. If you can't fix it, I will."

Kevin held Paul's even stare. He could see the determination in the set of his boss's jaw. Kevin could argue, but he knew he wouldn't win. Besides, there wasn't time for a major confrontation. "If that's it, I have to get going."

Paul's face relaxed, seeming relieved. "Just one more thing. No seminars or anything work-related. A *real* vacation." Kevin was halfway out the door when Paul called out, "Someplace warm, with women in bikinis."

"Yeah, yeah." In spite of himself, Kevin smiled over his shoulder. "I'll see what I can do."

He strode down the hall, raking his hair off his forehead, trying to feel annoyed with the chief, but not succeeding. Actually, a vacation didn't sound half-bad. Someplace warm, huh? Florida in April was out of the question. With his luck, he'd find himself in the middle of spring break and all those raging hormones. No, something more sedate, maybe farther south.

He pushed open the door to Recovery vowing to do two things on Saturday: get a haircut and visit a travel agency.

As long as he stayed in Recovery, his every thought remained with his patient. But a few minutes later, scrubbing for his second bypass surgery of the day, he let his mind drift back to the conversation with Paul. He despised being ordered around, anyone telling him when, where or what to do. But as the idea took root, he had to admit to feeling a certain amount of excitement. When was the last time he'd taken a real vacation? It had to be before Jessica....

*Damn.* He was doing it again. Measuring everything in terms of Jessica. Before she this. After she that.

With his sterile hands pointed to the ceiling, he pushed the operating room door open with his back. Later, he'd thank Paul for forcing this command down his throat. But for now, taking a closer look at the young mother of two on the table in front of him, he said a silent prayer, and put all other thoughts from his mind except this young patient and the precarious life he held in his hands.

* * *

For the next two weeks, Michelle worked with a vengeance, refusing to dwell on the calendar and the significance of each passing day.

It was Easter Sunday and she'd planned to go to St. Mary's for mass, then Greektown for breakfast. But at eight-thirty, as she looked out the seventh-floor window of her waterfront apartment, ice pelted against the glass and she changed her mind. The Detroit River and Windsor beyond hid behind a curtain of sleet and gray. A melancholy settled over her sparsely furnished apartment. It was too quiet. Too empty. She started a CD of Streisand's biggest hits and tightened her robe around her waist. Holidays were the toughest.

It'd been over two years since her parents' fatal accident, right on the heels of her divorce. As an only child, she'd grown up with a lot of time to herself, but never completely alone. The last Easter she spent with Mom and Dad, they'd still hidden bright-colored eggs all over their Traverse City home. And pretending to be too old for such games, she'd happily gathered them up, thinking the game would never end, that there would be many more Easters.

Michelle settled into the recliner facing the window, covered her legs with her mother's handmade afghan, and picked up a romance novel from the table alongside the chair. She read two chapters before she set the book down and stared out the frosty glass. Until this very moment, she hadn't admitted there was something else weighing on her mind. And it had nothing to do with the weather or missing her parents. It had everything to do with the mild cramping in her midsection. She threw back the afghan and marched to the bathroom, angry with herself for postponing the inevitable. A quick check would tell her whether her fears were substantiated.

They were.

Numb with disappointment, she dragged herself to the kitchen.

"Enough, Purdue." She swiped at a lone tear with the back of her hand and sniffled loudly, then slapped a filter into the coffee maker. While the brew dripped through, she found a yellow legal pad and pencil. A moment later, she poured her coffee and took everything to the table.

Making lists always empowered her; crossing things off gave her a sense of accomplishment. For the next hour she wrote out her plan . . . *Call clinic, make another appointment, continue taking temperature daily, log results, finish urgent jobs within two weeks, clear calendar for week following, call travel agent, make reservations for someplace warm. . . .*

She chewed the end of the pencil and lingered on the last entry. After the first insemination she'd buried herself in work to keep her mind occupied. Maybe the pace and tension had ruined whatever chances she'd had. This time she'd give her mind, as well as her body, a well-deserved break. But where should she go?

Restless, she pushed out of her chair and began pacing the small area from the table to the living room window, finally stopping at the window after half a dozen turns. The sleet had stopped. Windsor was now in clear view. Idly she watched cars making their way along the Detroit River on the Canadian side. Her apartment was small, the rent steep. But this was why she'd signed the lease. She never tired of the awe-inspiring view.

A freighter, low in the water, made its way down the river. Michelle watched it, wishing it was warmer and she was on it, feeling the sun and wind on her face.

That was it! That was what she'd do! Not a freighter but a cruise. She'd thought about it last January and even gone as far as picking up a few brochures.

Michelle raced for her computer workstation, nestled neatly in the corner of her bedroom. Opening a bottom drawer, she riffled through a stack of magazines and brochures until she found what she was looking for: Norwegian Cruise Line— ninety-three full-color pages with countless choices. She closed her eyes and pressed the glossy pages to her chest. She thought about the last year's worth of charts and temperatures. She'd been blessed with a fairly regular schedule. Only twice had she been late ovulating, and then merely by one or two days.

She grabbed her calendar and returned to the kitchen table. She did a quick calculation, then flipped through the pages looking at departure dates. There it was. The *Norway* departed Miami at 4:30 p.m., Saturday, April 15, which should be the third day of her fertile cycle. If she was late by two days she would still be fertile Saturday morning. Perfect.

Excited, she refilled her mug and returned her attention to the glossy pages in front of her. Tomorrow she'd call the travel agent and book passage. She'd heard there was usually last-minute space, sometimes at bargain prices. And she'd call Donna at the clinic and let her know she'd be back April 13th, 14th or 15th, depending on her temperature.

Michelle closed the brochure, a vague uneasiness creeping up her spine as she thought about Donna. After months of working with the young woman on the clinic's computer system, she'd thought she'd allayed all her concerns about using a sperm bank. But surprisingly, one small detail still bothered her—the unknown face of the donor, should her lucky day ever come. She sipped her coffee and tried shrugging off the thought, but the idea of a faceless father niggled away at her otherwise perfect plan. According to Donna, this was a common problem. She'd said some women found handsome men's photos—either in magazines or catalogs or the ones that came in frames—and pretended they were the daddies.

She leaned back and thought about it for a moment until a devilish idea tugged at the corners of her mouth. What if she found someone on the ship? Not a relationship. Just an affair of the heart with some perfect stranger . . . a face to remember if—no, *when* the time came she needed one.

Yesiree. A great plan. Later tonight, a little mood music and a glass of chardonnay, and she'd imagine the perfect face . . . and maybe the perfect body, too. Suddenly the cruise was taking on a whole new dimension, and the thought of it sent shivers of excitement down her spine. Next month everything would work out and today's disappointment would be history. She could almost smell the salty night air, feel the wind whipping her hair away from her moist neck, music drifting from a dance floor. . . .

# Two

At six o'clock Saturday morning, April 15, Michelle opened one eye and drew a bead on the waiting thermometer on the nightstand, hoping to instill a conscience into the unrelenting object. Both Thursday and Friday it had been a cold, heartless fiend. If it didn't cooperate today, she'd be faced with the choice of canceling her cruise or missing a fertile month. Somehow she doubted a letter from Dr. Adam would qualify as a medical emergency. She could kiss the cost of her airfare and the cruise goodbye. She reached for the thermometer, hoping it would save the day.

It did. Sort of. It read higher, but not as high as she'd expected. She stared at it a moment, wondering if it was high enough, then kissed its hard, pointy little head and logged the number on the chart. She should have purchased one of those ovulation indicator kits months ago, but it was too late now. Trying to remain calm and confident, she called the clinic and said she was on the way. Once she was there, they would test her and tell her everything was okay. Today was the big day.

* * *

At eight-forty-five Michelle eyed the clock on the dashboard. Her flight for Miami didn't leave until ten-fifty. Plenty of time. She eased up on the accelerator as she headed west on I-94 for Metro Airport.

She'd missed last night's stay at the Marriott in Miami that came with the trip, which meant she'd have to catch a cab directly to the ship. Then she'd have a couple of hours to rest in her cabin before departure. Michelle forced down the anxiety she felt pushing at her rib cage, willing herself to remain calm.

It had barely been an hour since the procedure and the doctor's words still hung over her like a dark cloud. *You're not ovulating yet.... Probably tomorrow... It would be better to wait....* But in the end he'd agreed that sperm could live a couple of days with a high count such as her donor's, and that as long as she ovulated soon, she still had a fairly good chance.

She turned the car radio to an easy-listening station and breathed deeply. Tomorrow at this time she'd be on the *Norway,* halfway to St. Martin and other ports of call. A weeklong cruise full of sunshine, fresh air and, best of all, no phones. All those odd-hour emergencies would somehow be handled by her clients. If all else failed, maybe they'd open their software manuals and figure things out for themselves. She frowned. If too many customers did that, would they need her when she got home? Finally she laughed and relaxed her grip on the steering wheel. Sometimes she worried about the silliest things.

She'd been free-lancing now for three years and had more referrals than she could handle. In fact, one of the changes she'd have to make before any baby arrived was to cut down on the sixty-hour workweeks. She exited the freeway at Merriman Road and headed for the terminal. The income was nice. It enabled her to take this cruise and pay for all the tests and trips to the clinic. But she didn't have to put in so much time anymore. Years of hard work and no frills, plus her parents' life insurance proceeds, had netted her a healthy nest egg.

"Humph!" She pulled up to the curb and flagged a skycap. Nest egg. Even her analogies were hormonal lately. *Tick, tick, tick.* It was so annoying. Thirty-six wasn't the end.

The skycap tagged her luggage and stapled receipts to her ticket. A couple of laps around the long-term parking lot and she found a spot. She grabbed her purse off the passenger seat and locked the car, annoyed with herself for growing harried. If she let the possibility of motherhood monopolize her thoughts for the next month, she'd go crazy. And if she wanted those little swimmers to live until tomorrow and have a chance at reaching their destination, she'd better forget about them and relax. With a new resolve, she exhaled loudly and strolled toward the terminal.

Shortly after two o'clock, Michelle followed the porter and her bags up the gangplank, a humid head wind slowing their pace. At seventy-six degrees, it was already twenty degrees warmer than home and the ship hadn't even left dock.

Michelle smiled. This had been the right decision. She had a good feeling about this trip. With any luck, a new life was already beginning inside her. And with the throngs of passengers leaning over railings and still boarding, certainly there had to be at least one handsome fantasy man among them.

They made their way up to the Viking Deck and aft to her stateroom, where the porter deposited her bags and promptly departed. A pair of portholes drew her to the far wall. She peered out and saw another ship making its way out of the harbor, waving arms visible from her many decks. On a satisfied sigh, Michelle turned and scanned the space around her. The room was small, but tastefully decorated. Actually, all she needed was clean and private. She didn't plan on spending much time in here, anyway. She placed her hands on her hips and wondered what to do next. What she usually did first when she traveled was unpack. What she probably should do was lie down and rest.

Neither seemed appealing.

Her stomach growled and she looked at her watch. She'd chosen late meal settings, which meant dinner wasn't until eight-thirty, more than six hours away. Sandwiches were supposed to be available near the pool, wherever that was.

She found a diagram of the ship and studied it a moment, getting her bearings. The pool was one level up, on the forward end of the Pool Deck. That seemed logical.

A moment later she pocketed her key and headed down the narrow hallway. It was all she could do to keep from laughing. The idea of cruising each deck in search of her fantasy man had already brought her hours of entertainment.

Now the game could actually begin.

She'd decided on blue eyes, dark hair, six-two or so, a rugged, tanned complexion and the body of an athlete. It might take her all week to find such a specimen, but hey, the looking would be half the fun.

Animated passengers swarmed around Le Bistro, plastic tumblers in one hand and paper plates in the other. Michelle pressed her way through the crowd, helped herself to a couple of tuna points, celery sticks and iced tea, then looked around for an empty seat. Finding none, she strolled back along the railing to the stairway and walked up a level. A quiet place where the sounds of the seas replaced the drum of the city was just what the doctor ordered. It was either that or go to her room and stand on her head in the corner. She'd heard some women actually did that to increase their chances....

*Damn.* She had to get her mind off this morning.

She turned to starboard and found a comfortable chaise longue. There she settled, placing her plate and tea on the table beside her.

With a celery stick between her lips, she took in the endless blue-green horizon, suddenly feeling very small, and that life's little foibles were insignificant. She finished her snack, her eyes never leaving the gently rolling waters. It was so hypnotic she felt her lids grow heavier and heavier, until finally she leaned back and closed her eyes.

A cool breeze stirred the salty air. Waves slapped steadily against the hull far below, each one by measure stripping away layers of tension, leaving her limbs languid, her mind afloat. Her last waking thought was that she might never leave this spot.

* * *

*HOOOHHHNNN... HOOOHHHNNN...*

The nasal blast reverberated through the ship and Michelle
sat up with a start. Looking left and right, she didn't see a soul.
Disoriented, she blinked rapidly, then remembered where she
was.

She pulled herself awake and followed the hoopla coming
from the other side, half expecting the ship to list—like in that
coffee commercial she'd seen. She smiled at her own private
joke as she rounded the corner. The elbow-to-elbow crowd was
covered with confetti and streamers tossed from above. At first
glance, the scene seemed too contrived for her tastes. It reminded her of plastic leis at backyard luaus. But apparently her
attitude wasn't shared.

She scanned the noisy crowd until she spotted the only other
uninvolved figure. He was leaning on his forearms, looking like
a poised cat amid a field of scurrying mice. In contrast to the
riotous tourist garb that surrounded him, he wore a light blue
button-down shirt and darker blue Dockers pants. His thick
chestnut hair was cropped short, a breeze lifting a few strands
from his pale forehead. While he was lean, he didn't have the
look of an athlete, and he certainly wasn't someone who spent
much time outdoors.

Below, the mighty engines toiled and vibrated as the ship
pulled slowly from the dock.

Still, the man didn't move.

And neither did Michelle.

She noticed the older couple to his right were still waving toward shore, smiling and chatting among themselves. The young
couple on his left wrapped their arms around each other and
hugged. The man in the middle looked like an island unto
himself, staring straight ahead, his posture not encouraging
conversation. He didn't fit the profile of her fantasy man, but
nonetheless, something held her attention.

He straightened and turned his back to the railing and
Michelle continued her assessment. About six feet tall, around
forty, square jaw, dark eyes—though at this distance she
couldn't be sure of their color. She squinted and tried harder to
see. Suddenly there was a dimple between his brows and he
folded his arms across his chest.

*Oh, God.* He was looking right at her. She'd been caught—
ogling him like a woman on the prowl. Heat crept up her neck
and she spun on her heel. As quickly as she could, she walked
back the way she'd come and out of sight before exhaling the
breath she'd been holding.

*Whew!* She'd have to be more discreet in the future, she lectured herself, heading for the stairway. But for now, she'd give
up the game and unpack. Then she'd take a shower and change
for dinner. Later, she'd take a stroll and resume her search.


Kevin stood there and stared. He watched the sun play on the
woman's copper ponytail until it sashayed out of sight.

Now what was that all about? he wondered, turning and
walking in the opposite direction. Was this what he was in for
all week? Single women looking for unattached males? Or
maybe that one had just watched too many reruns of "Love
Boat." Either way, he'd keep to himself and watch what he
said. One thing was certain. He wouldn't let on he was a doctor. Why women found that a turn-on, he'd never understand.
How many birthday dinners or concerts or parties had he been
dragged away from for a patient's needs? Unless it was the
money, he couldn't imagine what attracted them.

He stopped and looked down at the water churning below.
He'd thought Jessica understood the long hours and constant
interruptions. Apparently, she hadn't.

Jessica. She'd always wanted to take a cruise, but he'd forever been too busy. *Damn.* When was he going to stop beating
himself up over the past? He walked on, staring blindly at his
loafers. Maybe this trip had been a mistake.


After changing her mind three times, Michelle settled on a
silk pantsuit. The pants were cut full, the top long. The water-
color fabric in soft shades of fern green complemented her
burnished hair, which she wore down tonight, the blunt-cut
ends brushing her shoulders.

She stood back from the mirror behind the door and made a
final inspection. Even with low-heeled pumps, she thought she
looked taller than her five feet five inches. The fact that she'd
lost ten pounds since Christmas added to the long, clean lines
of her outfit. Months of swimming and water aerobics had paid

off. Without thinking, her hand moved over her flat stomach. She could probably get away with clothes like this for several months.

She jerked her hand away and turned from the mirror. It was too soon to think this way. It was one thing to think positive, but if she continued to assume it was a done deal, she could be setting herself up for a major disappointment.

She looked at the small clutch purse on the bed, then decided to leave it behind. There was no need for money, and if her lipstick wore off, oh, well . . .

The Windward Dining Room was midship, two levels down. Michelle sauntered along the halls and stairway, marveling at the architectural splendor—teak rails, hand-laid tile mosaics, marble statuary, art deco murals. A person could get used to this. At the entrance to the dining room, Michelle retrieved her seat assignment card from her pants pocket and handed it to the tuxedo-clad maître d'.

She followed him up the right side, weaving her way through the lively crowd, losing sight of him toward the end. She kept moving and found him again, standing behind an empty chair at a rectangular table for six. On the side facing her she saw a young couple who had the starry-eyed look of honeymooners, seated next to a kind-faced, blue-haired woman of about seventy. Across from her she could see the back of another woman about the same age who looked as if she'd visited the same beautician. Next to her was a man. In the few seconds it took to reach her seat, she couldn't figure out where he fit in.

Michelle's chair was no sooner pushed in than the young man in front of her extended his hand across the table.

"Welcome aboard. I'm Mark, and this is my beautiful bride, Kathy."

Kathy elbowed her husband and giggled before lowering her lashes. "We just got married last night," she said shyly.

"Congratulations!" Enjoy it while you can, she wanted to add but didn't. "I'm Michelle." She clasped each of their hands in turn.

The older woman spoke next, her gaze lingering on the new bride beside her. "Isn't it romantic?" Then she turned her attention to Michelle. "My name's Millie, and this is my sister Hazel." Millie's head shook involuntarily, reminding Michelle of Katharine Hepburn's later years. "Nice to meet you, Michelle." Too far to reach, both women offered friendly waves with bejeweled freckled hands.

"Nice to meet you both." Michelle could see the mischief dancing in their eyes, not certain what they were up to, but deciding instantly she liked the pair.

Millie laced her fingers in front of her chest and smiled expectantly. "Michelle, allow me to introduce our new friend sitting next to you."

Michelle turned sideways in her seat, her smile still on Millie who was obviously enjoying herself immensely. Finally Michelle faced the stranger to her right. He turned his head slowly, his square jaw and gray eyes scant inches away.

*Oh, no. It couldn't be.*

But it was.

She knew a blush had turned her cheeks crimson, but she could do nothing to hide it. Fighting the urge to get up and run, she held out her hand as Millie finished.

"His name is Kevin. I always liked that name. And now with Kevin Costner and all...well, well..." She fanned herself and the others laughed. All but Kevin, who held Michelle's gaze and didn't smile.

"Kevin?" She hadn't meant for it to sound like a question, but it came out that way.

"Michelle?" He cocked an eyebrow and mocked her response. She was about to drop her hand when he finally took it in his. "And so we meet again."

"Oh! You two already know each other?" Millie asked.

Michelle pulled her hand back and straightened in her chair. "Not exactly. We just...saw each other on deck earlier."

Millie pushed on. "We haven't had much time to get acquainted, but Kevin told us he isn't married. Are you, Michelle?"

Hazel reached across the table and slapped her sister's hand. "Really, Millie. You can be such a busybody."

Michelle took a sip of water and kept her eyes on the glass. "No, I'm not," she said quietly, not wanting to underscore her answer.

*Oh, God.* A whole week of sharing meals with this man. How would she ever explain her earlier actions?

The waiter came and asked if anyone cared for a cocktail. What she'd give for a good stiff drink. But after this morning's visit to the clinic, she'd sworn off alcohol just in case...

"And you, ma'am? Would you care for something?"

"I'll have a Virgin Mary, please."

Kevin started to laugh, then turned it into a cough and drank some water.

She wanted to turn on him and ask, "What's your problem?" but she kept her face forward and smiled at the newlyweds, who had all but forgotten everyone else at the table.

Millie and Hazel kept up a running commentary on the menu until orders were taken. Then, later, between dainty bites of food, they educated the table on the history of the ship.

"She was originally called the *S.S. France,* you know," Millie said.

"Did you know she's as long as the Eiffel Tower is tall?" Hazel asked the group. Heads shook and the pair prattled on, no one seeming to mind, though Michelle hadn't a clue what Kevin's expression was. She hadn't looked at him once since the introduction.

When it was time for dessert, Michelle pushed out her chair and stood. "It was very nice meeting all of you, but I think I'm going to call it a night."

"Oh, so soon?" Millie pulled an exaggerated frown.

"I think we will, too." Mark looked into Kathy's eyes and she nuzzled closer to his side.

"Until tomorrow." Michelle forced a smile and turned left, purposefully avoiding eye contact with Kevin. She walked away, back straight, gait slow. From the rear, she hoped she appeared relaxed and unruffled. Inside, she wanted to scream and run from the room.

Why did he have to be at *her* table?

Leaving the dining room, she quickened her pace to her room. Once inside, she kicked off her shoes and dropped onto the bed.

And why did he have to be so damnably good-looking? And *Kevin,* no less.

She closed her eyes and recalled his reaction when they'd met. What was it she'd seen in the brief moment she allowed herself to look him in the eye? Disdain? Arrogance? Curiosity? She couldn't be sure. It had happened so fast and so unexpectedly.

Michelle inhaled deeply and blew out slowly. Relax. She had to relax. She stretched out on her back and stared at the ceiling.

"Okay. So it was embarrassing," she said aloud. "Now what?"

She could ask for a new seat assignment, but then how would she explain it to Millie and Hazel and the newlyweds? Millie would certainly seek her out and ask why she'd moved. Besides, she liked these people. New table companions could be a lot worse.

No. She'd stay put.

So what about Kevin? She could *A,* explain her actions, or *B,* ignore it and hope things smoothed over.

She thought a moment about *A.* How would she explain? *Well, you see Kevin, I was artificially inseminated this morning and I was looking for a certain face to use for the fantasy father... yada, yada, yada.*

Right. He'd probably swallow that.

*B* it was. She'd look him in the eye, whenever necessary, and pretend nothing happened.

Michelle pushed off the bed, undressed and went about her nightly routine. Having decided she'd have the breakfast buffet on deck instead of at the table, she found her romance novel and climbed naked between the cool sheets.

Puffing a second pillow behind her head, she found her place and began to read.

*She gazed into his steely gray eyes, and in that fleeting moment she knew he was the one....*

Michelle slammed the book shut and turned out the light.

# Three

___

**D**awn crept through the twin portholes above Michelle's bed, and she stretched languorously. The gentle rocking of the ship had cradled her into a dreamless sleep, leaving her more rested than she'd felt in years. It wasn't yet seven, but her stomach was growling and she longed for some coffee.

She threw herself into gear, eager for the feel of ocean breezes. Breakfast on deck sounded heavenly. And it meant postponing dealing with Kevin, too. A little food and a good book. That would tide her over for a while. Later, she'd resume her search for the fantasy father, but with more finesse than yesterday.

After a quick shower, she pulled her hair into a ponytail and donned a pair of white shorts and a white T-shirt. So what if it wasn't after Memorial Day? She was on vacation and so were the old rules. With her book tucked securely under her arm, she left her stateroom and strode down the hall, the salty scent growing stronger with each long stride.

At the top of the stairs, she followed the aroma of fresh brewed coffee, surprised to find a number of early risers already in line at the buffet tables near the pool. Goose bumps rose on her bare arms and legs and she wished she'd dressed warmer. She spotted an empty table in the sun. Helping herself to coffee and juice, she headed toward it. She deposited her beverages and book, then joined the line for food, all the while gazing out over the endless sea.

The line inched forward at a turtle's pace, which for a change didn't bother her in the least. There was no client waiting, no place she had to be. Smiling at a pair of lovers strolling by, she took another step forward.

And ran right into the person in front of her.

Michelle jumped back. "Excuse me. I'm so sorry."

At the sound of her voice, Kevin turned abruptly. "You!"

Openmouthed, Michelle stared up at him, not liking the acerbic tone he'd so easily adopted. She jutted out her chin and took the offensive. "Are you following me?"

His laugh was low and sardonic. "You're the one behind me, Michelle." He leaned heavily on her name. "Look, maybe we should get something straight up front. I'm not interested." He'd started to turn back when she grabbed his arm.

"And what makes you think I am?" The words were no sooner out than she knew the answer.

Kevin cocked his head and arched an accusatory eyebrow.

"If you're talking about that departure incident, don't flatter yourself. I was watching something behind you. I didn't even notice you until you started staring at me," she lied, with more aplomb than she'd known she had in her.

"Right." He dropped an English muffin on his plate and turned his back on her.

Of all the pompous, arrogant... Her breathing was rapid, her face hot. She searched for a clever retort, but was too embarrassed and angry to think.

Michelle slapped food onto her plate, barely taking stock of her choices. Well, she *could* have been looking at something behind him. How did he know?

Kevin wandered off in the opposite direction as she rushed over to her table. She positioned her chair away from the crowd and faced the railing, then dropped heavily into it.

Men! No wonder she was still single—a fact that sounded better every day.

Michelle munched on a piece of rye toast as her breathing returned to normal. What was wrong with her? It was a gorgeous day and she was on her way to a tropical island. There were about two thousand people on this ship. She couldn't let one insolent man ruin it all. She drank her coffee, feeling its warmth trickle through her, then picked up her book. One thing was certain. She'd have lunch outside, too, and be sure he was nowhere in sight when she approached the buffet. Tonight she'd deal with Mr. God's Gift.

Michelle read the same page twice before closing her eyes and lifting her face to the sun. Damn, but he was good-looking. That probably accounted for the attitude. Poor baby—getting hit on at every turn.

A slow smile tugged at the corners of her mouth. Maybe she should give him a little of what he expected. Why not? If he didn't like it, *he* could ask for a new table and the problem would be solved.


Kevin tightened the knot on his tie, buttoned down the points of his collar and mumbled under his breath. He'd spent the better part of the day peering around corners for that ever-present redhead, not once spotting her. Had he been wrong about her looking for action, or had he just been lucky not to run into her again? He slipped on his navy blue pinstripe suit coat and stepped away from the mirror. It wasn't a tux, but it would have to do. He wasn't about to put on a monkey suit just to meet the captain of the ship. In fact, he didn't see a need to stand in some long line to shake the guy's hand, either. What a strange custom. How many pilots had travelers met? This was simply a bigger ship. He shrugged and left the room. Guess it made as much sense as throwing confetti overboard.

Maybe Paul was right. He'd lost his sense of humor. Everyone else had seemed caught up in the departure ritual. All but Michelle, he remembered, as he entered the dining room and pressed his way through sequins and satin. Maybe he'd been wrong about her. If she hadn't changed tables, he'd do his best to make amends.

Across the room he spotted Millie and Hazel already seated,
along with the lovebirds. They'd all assumed the same places.
It reminded him of the one time he'd served on jury duty. The
jurors had always taken the same seats in the deliberation room.
He wondered what havoc he'd wreak if he sat in a different
chair. The only one left now was Michelle's. If he wanted to
start fresh with the woman, that probably wasn't the way to
begin. Millie waved excitedly as he approached.

"My, don't you ladies look gorgeous!" he said. They did,
each in their own way. "I guess I'm a little underdressed."

"You look very handsome, Kevin." Millie smiled coyly, then
lowered her gaze. Hazel reached over and patted his hand reassuringly. Maybe they thought he couldn't afford formal attire, which was just as well. He'd hate to think how much more
active their obvious matchmaking efforts would be if they knew
the truth.

"Did you meet Captain Olson?" Hazel asked.

"No, I'm afraid I didn't."

"Sis and I arrived early and were near the front of the line.
He's *soooo* charming, don't you think, Millie?"

"Oh, yes." She hunched her narrow shoulders and wiggled
them. "I've always loved a man in uniform, all epaulets and
braid, every crease to perfection." She winked at Kevin and he
couldn't help but smile. "Kevin, tell us about your day—" Her
gaze suddenly left his as she stopped in midsentence and stared
openmouthed at the space behind his left shoulder. "Oh, my,
my, my!"

Curious, Kevin turned in his chair, his face just inches away
from ample cleavage squeezed firmly in place by a shimmering
silver strapless gown. His jaw dropped as his gaze traveled
north, stopping at the most beautiful green eyes he'd ever seen.
"Michelle?" His voice cracked like an adolescent's.

She held out her hand to him. "Kevin?"

He didn't miss the instant replay of their first meeting, but
he was too dumbstruck for a clever retort. He didn't know
whether to shake her hand or kiss it. Instead, he held on to it
and stood up, his gaze never leaving hers.

Finally he closed his mouth and pulled out her chair. She sat
gracefully, then eyed him evenly when he rejoined the table.

"Thank you, Kevin," she said with a smile. "It's a lovely evening, isn't it?"

He nodded, not sure what to make of this poised and polite stranger beside him. Could this possibly be the same creature who had nearly assaulted him at breakfast, deserved as that might have been?

"Did you enjoy your day at sea?" she asked, still smiling.

Not really. He'd wasted most of it trying to avoid her. Why—looking at her now—he hadn't a clue. Before he could answer, Hazel leaned in and talked around him.

"I love your hair that way, dear. Did you do it yourself?"

Kevin looked at the burnished curls swept atop her head, a few strategic tendrils gracing her temples and long neck. He could picture her in a whirlpool full of bubbles with her hair like that, the ends wet above those perfect bare shoulders. An alarm went off in his head and he looked away.

"No," Michelle answered. "I treated myself to the works today. Hair, nails, even a massage—which I highly recommend. It was heavenly."

Millie's eyebrows shot up. "Masseur or masseuse?"

"Millie!" Hazel sent a warning glare, but Michelle found the question amusing and laughed.

"It was a woman," she answered.

"Oh." Millie seemed disappointed.

Kevin felt relieved. Though he wasn't sure why he should care.

Millie shifted her attention back to him. "Now, Kevin. You were about to tell us about your day."

He shrugged. "Not much to tell. I read a little, walked a lot. And you two?"

Hazel burst in. "We won a hundred and fifty dollars between us at the blackjack tables. It was so exciting."

"Of course, we lost most of it at the roulette wheel, but it was fun anyway," Millie added.

Kevin noticed no one asked the honeymooners about their day. There were whisker burns on the bride's neck, and their lips looked like recent collagen recipients. Go for it, he thought and smiled. You never know how long . . .

The waiter appeared and took drink orders, cutting into his petulant thoughts. This time, when Michelle ordered a Virgin Mary he didn't laugh. Apparently she wasn't much of a drinker. Later, when the groom ordered a bottle of champagne for the table, Kevin noticed she still refrained. For a fleeting moment, he wondered if she was a reformed alcoholic, but then he let the suspicion pass. With a body like hers, she was probably a health nut. When dessert was served and she waved it off, he remembered she hadn't eaten any last night, either. Nothing wrong with that, he decided. He'd seen enough clogged arteries to appreciate a good diet.

Millie wiped her mouth daintily with the corner of her napkin before speaking. "Hazel and I were thinking of going to... to... What was the name of it, dear?"

"Checkers Cabaret."

"That's it. They're supposed to have exotic coffees and after-dinner drinks...plus music for dancing." Kevin noticed her gaze darted between him and Michelle, a hopeful expression on her frail little face. He lifted his champagne glass and stalled hoping Michelle would answer first, which she did.

"I think I'll just take a stroll around deck and then call it a night," she said. "But thanks for asking, ladies. Maybe another time." She pushed out her chair and stood, the slit up her right side exposing a well-formed thigh sheathed in silky sheer hose.

Kevin tried not to stare, but he knew she caught his glance.

Hazel said, "Maybe we'll run into each other at the shore excursion desk tomorrow." She looked up at Michelle. "You are going to St. Martin Tuesday, aren't you, dear?"

Michelle clutched the back of her chair and smiled demurely. "I don't think so. Unless I change my mind, I was thinking of staying aboard." The sisters moaned in perfect unison. "I've been to St. Martin before, but this is my first cruise," Michelle added. "I thought I might enjoy roaming the ship when it wasn't so crowded."

Millie was now staring at Kevin, who refused to take the bait. He didn't know what he would be doing ten minutes from now, let alone day after tomorrow. Right now, a walk with Michelle had its appeal, but not under the close scrutiny of the well-

intentioned matchmakers. They didn't need any encourage-
ment.

"Can you dance, Kevin?" Hazel asked unexpectedly.

"Well, I . . ."

"Of course he can!" Millie scurried around the table,
beaming from diamond-studded ear to diamond-studded ear.
"I get the first waltz, Hazel," she called over her shoulder,
tugging him from his chair.

"Oh, Millie. Don't be silly. I bet they don't even play a
waltz." They each claimed an arm and continued their banter
as if it were a sure thing he would join them.

Kevin smiled down on the pair of bobbing blue heads and let
them lead him away. One dance each and then he'd leave,
hopefully before Michelle finished her walk.

Forty minutes later, longer than he had planned, Kevin excused himself and took the stairs two at a time to the Sky Deck,
then systematically made his way around and down each level.
But no slender redhead graced the railing. Finally, he gave up
and headed for his stateroom, disappointment and relief warring inside his gut. Who was this woman, anyway? And worse
yet, why did he suddenly care?

Tuesday morning Michelle found an empty chair on the Sun
Deck and finished the dregs of her coffee. It was nearly noon
and for hours she'd watched tender after tender transport excited passengers ashore. Earlier she'd wondered if she'd made
a bad decision staying behind, but now, bathed in sun and se-
renity, she wasn't sorry.

With the side of her hand shielding her eyes she studied the
private yachts dotting the seascape. One in particular caught
her eye. It was anchored far from shore, away from the others, and had to be at least a hundred feet long. Lifting her binoculars from around her neck, she adjusted the focus and
slowly swept the ship's length. She was about to drop the lenses
when a sole figure appeared on the fan tail. A bearded man
dressed in a tartan plaid kilt, of all things. Fascinated, she
watched and waited. He hoisted something over his head and
positioned a strap across his shoulder and chest, tucking a large

bag beneath his upper arm. When he began blowing into a tube, Michelle knew her first guess had been correct.

Bagpipes.

She lowered the glasses and moved to the railing, anticipation racing through her veins. Before the melody began, she knew she was in for a treat. But when the first haunting refrain of "Amazing Grace" wafted toward her, she wasn't prepared for the emotion it evoked. A favorite since childhood, the poignant tune began spinning its web about her. Transfixed, she stared at the source of the magic, the words forming on her lips without sound. It felt as though he played just for her. Each high-pitched note wailed and lingered until the next, weaving a mystical spell around her soul. God was talking to her—what the message, she wasn't sure, but the power and passion were like none she'd ever known. The Caribbean was her cathedral. And hers alone.

Even the footsteps behind her didn't break her concentration. When the person stopped beside her she remained riveted, wishing the music would never stop, hoping whoever joined her would possess the sensitivity not to speak. Tears trailed down her hot cheeks, but she did nothing to hide them, fearing the slightest movement might break the spell.

With only the slightest pause, the tune began again. She closed her eyes and felt her body sway with the gentle rocking of the ship. And then a new sound pierced the stillness beside her. In one of the most beautiful tenor voices she'd ever heard, the words she mouthed came soft yet clear from the person at her side. His intonation returned the soulful tune with as much meaning and tenderness as its sender.

Michelle gripped the railing, her legs trembling from sensual saturation. And when the last note faded into nothingness, she felt both sad and relieved, the intensity of the experience one she would never be able to explain to another human being.

Except maybe this man beside her. But then words were inadequate.

Minutes passed in total silence. Still, she didn't move. Nor did he. She wanted to sit down before her legs buckled, but should she turn away from him without comment? Or did she turn toward him? Suddenly she felt vulnerable—an unfamiliar and uncomfortable feeling. She'd let someone see a part of her she wasn't sure she'd ever seen herself. Better to have been caught in the buff than to expose her soul.

Finally, gathering all the courage she could muster, she turned toward him. His eyes were shiny, his cheeks damp. And he was gazing down at her like a vision from heaven.

"Kevin," she whispered, surprised yet somehow relieved. He took her hand, but didn't speak. They turned back to the railing and gazed out at the yacht, her deck now deserted. For a moment Michelle wondered if the bagpipes had been real, but then Kevin squeezed her hand ever so gently, telegraphing a message only the two of them could understand.

Others began wandering over to the railing, speculating on what they'd heard moments earlier. Still holding her hand, Kevin led her away from the crowd, their steps measured, trancelike. When they reached the stairs they descended in silence, then strolled leisurely down the Fjord Deck. Lifeboats lined the perimeter, partially obstructing the view. Apparently the few travelers who remained aboard preferred better spots. But to Michelle this was perfect. It provided time and space to think about what just happened.

When the bagpipes first began, she'd been happy to experience the moment alone, resenting the intrusion of someone else. But when Kevin opened his mouth and sang, the magic had taken on new heights and her spirit soared like never before.

Michelle slowed her pace so that she was barely moving and Kevin followed suit. Was there a message in this somewhere? Could God be trying to tell her how much happier life would be if shared with the right person?

She quickened her pace. Where was that old cynical Michelle who doubted the existence of Mr. Right?

But at this very moment, she was so filled with love and peace she couldn't help but think kindly of this man beside her. Was he merely a symbol of what she could have if she opened her heart and took another chance? Or was Kevin . . .

*No.* She shook her head, the last of the cocoon evaporating and reality seeping in. Without breaking stride and in a voice that sounded as if she'd just awoken, Michelle finally braved a few words. "Do you sing in church?"

They kept walking. Both looked straight ahead.

Kevin's answer seemed tentative, cautious. "No. I wish I could, but I'm usually working Sunday mornings. I used to sing in the men's choir in college, though. Now I'm lucky if I have time in the shower."

Michelle smiled as they rounded the corner and sauntered on. She liked this new Kevin. "What kind of work keeps you so busy Sunday mornings?"

At last he stopped and turned toward her, looking relaxed and self-assured. "What do you think I do? Take a guess."

She lifted the hand still in hers and studied it. "It's so clean and soft, no calluses. Definitely white-collar." She looked up into his magnetic gray eyes and her pulse quickened.

"So far so good," he said, his steady gaze saying so much more. "Could you be more specific?"

Michelle looked back to his hand in hers, its warmth now traveling up her arm. A part of her wanted to tell him what profession she'd pegged him in two days ago at the breakfast buffet, but she didn't feel that way now. Unfortunately, her thoughts betrayed her and she felt the corners of her mouth tug upward.

"Go ahead. Tell me. It's obviously amusing."

"Two days ago I was sure you were a lawyer."

He chuckled softly, his breath warm against her forehead. "And now?" he asked.

She braved a glance upward. "Now I'm sure you're not." He smiled, more with the corners of his eyes than his mouth.

"Why's that?"

*Because I saw your soul and lawyers don't have one.* But she couldn't bring herself to say that. "Because...because..." She held his steady gaze as the distance closed between them. He didn't seem interested in her answer. His soft lips pressed against her forehead and words disappeared, lost on a wave of emotion that left her trembling against him. He drew her closer until her cheek pressed his T-shirt. His soap and musky aftershave filled her nostrils while his hands circled her back, slowly, soothingly.

"I don't know about you, but I came on this cruise to get away from work." His breath brushed across her ear. "Do we have to talk about our jobs?"

They had better talk about something, Michelle thought. Soon. What had started as a spiritual experience had quickly become sensual, sending messages to long-forgotten parts of her.

She stepped back and forced a casual smile. "Why don't we make up something? And where we're from, too."

He slid his hands down her arms, then clasped her fingers in his. "Why not? Could be fun." The corners of his eyes crinkled, his gaze warm and steady. "I've always loved San Francisco."

"Really? So have I. Could we be from the same place?" He squeezed her hands and she felt the simple gesture travel up her arms and to her chest.

"A nice coincidence, don't you think?" He dropped one hand and started to stroll along the deck, still holding tight to the other. "So what do you do in San Francisco, Michelle?"

She walked on, matching his relaxed stride, and thought for a moment. "I'm in the medical field." She thought she felt him stiffen, but then he smiled down at her.

"Doing exactly what?" he asked.

"I . . . I, uh . . . I'm a nurse at a hospital." She liked this idea and decided to elaborate. "I work mostly with babies in the nursery. Sometimes in Pediatrics." Kevin stopped walking, propped his elbows on the railing, and stared at the water. Had she said something wrong? He suddenly seemed a million miles away. When he didn't speak, she asked, "And what do you do?"

He heaved a sigh and turned his back to the railing, avoiding her curious stare. "Let's see." He took a moment, then looked at her, seeming relaxed again. "I'm a general contractor. I restore old homes. There were some beautiful Victorians damaged in the last big quake that are still in need of repair." He took her hand and began to walk again. "It keeps me busy."

If she hadn't known this was a game, she'd have believed him. There was something traditional, even old-fashioned, in his demeanor that lent credence to his story. She liked their little charade, but suddenly she felt compelled to clear up their murky meeting. "About that departure scene . . ."

He stopped and faced her. "I sure jumped to the wrong conclusion, didn't I?"

"I really wasn't looking to meet someone—"

"I was rude to you at breakfast the next morning—"

"I thought you were a . . . a—"

"A real jerk?"

She smiled. "Probably better than what you thought I was." His laugh was low and easy. "And to think I almost—"

"—asked for another table?" Kevin finished for her. "Me too. How about if we start over?" He extended his hand and straightened his back in mock formality. "My name's Kevin."

Michelle clasped his hand in hers. "I'm Michelle. Nice meeting you, Kevin."

"Would you care to accompany me to lunch? I know of this perfect table."

Michelle emitted a nervous chuckle. His hand was still on hers—a fact that was both comfortable and unsettling at the same time. "I'd love to, Kevin." She extracted her hand, only for him to bend her arm in his.

They strolled on, with Michelle all too aware of the muscular arm that occasionally brushed the side of her breast.

# Four

When they approached the table a few minutes later, they chose different seats on opposite sides, then sat and stared at the menu selections. They avoided eye contact for several minutes, until the waiter took their orders and removed their props. Now Michelle let her gaze travel slowly to his, her heart thudding beneath her sundress. She couldn't remember the last time she'd felt this way around a man. And she wasn't sure she liked it. It wasn't part of her plan at all. Making peace with this stranger was one thing; getting hot and bothered was quite another.

"Do you swim?" Kevin asked, seeming unaware of her musings.

"Y-yes," she stammered. "Nothing too serious, though. Just like to play around . . . in the water," she finished quickly, feeling like a babbling fool.

"I noticed you had a book with you the other day. After lunch, why don't we put on our suits, catch up on our reading and hang out at the pool for a while?"

She just stared at him, thinking of the skimpy new bikini in her room.

"Unless you'd rather have the afternoon to yourself..."

"No," she practically shouted. Then finding a remnant of poise, she started again. "No. Your idea sounds perfect."

Lunch was served and she turned her attention to her chicken salad and melon, grateful when Kevin filled in the spaces with idle talk of the ship and the weather. He truly was a kind and interesting man.

And so good-looking.

Each time she met his steely gray eyes, she thought he could read her mind. If she didn't find the old cynical Michelle pretty damn quick, he was certain to revert to his original opinion of her.

How she finished her meal and found her cabin, she wasn't quite sure. But now, standing in front of the mirror, appraising her chartreuse bikini, she wondered how she'd get through the afternoon without making a total fool of herself. How could she act poised around him dressed like this? A shudder coursed through her as she wrapped herself in a white cotton cover-up and slipped into a pair of sandals. Halfway out the door she remembered her book and went back for it, stopping to look at the half-naked clinch scene on its cover. Rolling her eyes, she exhaled a loud breath and made her way down the hall and toward the Pool Deck.

In navy blue swim trunks, Kevin stood sideways in front of the mirror and sucked in his stomach. He didn't look heavy, he decided. Just a little soft. How long had it been since he'd played racquetball with Paul? All work and no play. Paul was right. He'd become a dull and out-of-shape body mechanic.

He turned back to the sink and leaned straight-armed against the vanity. Paul had been right about many things. He did need a vacation, as well as a change in attitude.

But was he ready for the next step? The mere idea of *dating* balled a knot of anxiety in his stomach. With Jessica it had been easy. It had been lust at first sight. He'd been just a kid, and he'd never given romance a thought. They'd met on campus.

studied together, hung out at the student union and copulated like rabbits.

He lifted his head and stared into the mirror. Next year he'd turn forty. He knew less about women now than he'd thought he did in school.

He pushed off the counter and paced the small quarters. Michelle was intelligent, witty and . . . and . . . okay, beautiful. The face and body he had tried to ignore. Unsuccessfully.

Was that the attraction? After all, it had been over four years since . . .

He stopped pacing. Wait a minute. He'd only held her hand. There was a big chasm between hand-holding and . . .

This train of thought was crazy. He didn't know a thing about this woman. Even if he did, that wouldn't mean she was interested in him. And what about sexually transmitted diseases? He'd never even *bought* a condom, let alone *used* one.

He pulled a T-shirt over his head, shoved a newspaper under his arm and practically ran from the room.

"Slow down, man," he grumbled under his breath.

Grace under fire. That was what he needed. He drew on it every day in the operating room. Where was it now?


Michelle read the same page for the third time, trying again to concentrate on the words in front of her. Finally, she shoved the bookmark into place and laid the novel aside. She tugged at her cover-up, checking that nothing provocative was exposed, just as she spotted Kevin approaching. She wished his white body was a turnoff, but as he strode confidently toward her, his commanding posture and lean physique made her stomach do another somersault.

"Is this seat for me?" he asked, smiling down at her.

"I haven't had a better offer." Michelle gestured for him to join her, doing her best to match his casual air.

"It doesn't look like you've been in the water yet," he said, looking her over.

"No. Not hot enough to tempt me yet." Poor choice of words. And a lie, to boot. It could be twenty degrees cooler and she'd still be feeling this unyielding heat.

But the idea of removing her cover-up and displaying her body seemed about as appealing as jumping overboard. The chartreuse bikini had seemed like a good idea after a week at the tanning salon. Now she was sure it would look like a neon sign that shouted, Take Me, Take Me.

Michelle looked out of the corner of her eye. Kevin had unfolded his paper and was reading the business section, oblivious to her discomfort. She reached for her book, if for no other reason than to provide a prop for her unsteady hands.

She flipped the page pretending to read. A moment later she turned another one, the silence becoming unbearable. She couldn't see what had captured his interest. It must be an engrossing article since he hadn't turned the page once. Finally, she gave up the pretense of reading and sauntered over to the pool. Still covered, she sat gingerly on the edge and dangled her legs over the side. The water was warm yet refreshing. If Kevin wasn't behind her, she'd shrug out of the cover and slide in.

But in a flash he wasn't behind her. Without moving her head, she watched his long legs slip into the water next to her.

Whose idea was this, anyway? Spending the afternoon with this . . . this handsome, eyes-of-steel, male person. She let her breath out slowly, trying not to show her anxiety.

He splashed water in front of him with his feet, still not saying a word. Just when she thought she couldn't take the silence another moment, he spoke.

"What are you hiding beneath that white thing?" He turned his head and she caught his devilish smile. "Midriff bulge or an appendix scar?"

Michelle straightened her back. "Neither. I . . . I didn't want to get sunburned."

He arched a disbelieving eyebrow. "Okay. Leave it on."

That did it. She never could back down from a challenge. Implied or otherwise.

As with removing a bandage, she decided fast was best. She stood, untied the sash, dropped the cover and dived into the tepid water. Doing a perfectly clean crawl, she swam the distance of the pool and back to Kevin before stopping for air.

Her chest was heaving rhythmically below the surface. Kevin was staring at her openmouthed, his gaze at water level.

"Nice...stroke," he said, his eyes eventually straying north.

She caught her breath. "Want to race?" At least it was something physical that wouldn't get her in trouble.

"I don't know." He cocked his head to one side and smiled. "You'd probably win. I'm not in the best of shape."

"I noticed." She smiled back before diving deep, coming up near the far end. When she turned and swung her wet hair from her face, he was inches away, his smooth freestyle carrying him past her and to the wall.

With elbows hooked over the edge he eyed her as she came alongside. "How many laps?" he asked.

His breathing was already labored. This would be a piece of cake. She glanced to the opposite end, then back to his challenging smirk. "How does five sound?" She fully expected him to protest.

He took a couple of deep breaths and exhaled loudly. "I'm ready when you are."

She positioned her hands and feet behind her, gave him one last look, then shouted, "Go!"

They started with a flurry, arms flying. Right, left. Right, left. Kevin was half a length in front of her.

No big deal. So he was a sprinter. She was a long-distance runner.

She let him set the pace, purposefully holding back, measuring her energy. He wouldn't be able to keep it up. Let him have his ego intact a little longer.

Michelle pushed off the wall as he came out of his turn and stayed with him through laps two and three and into four. Finally, he slowed his pace, his arms chopping instead of slicing through the water, less splash on his kick.

Keeping her same steady rhythm, she pulled alongside, then passed him on the last turn. He was gassed. No doubt about it. But then her own lungs were begging for relief, too.

She could do it. Just half a lap. God, her legs were tired. They felt like dead weights pulling her down. She slowed slightly, gliding the distance with each stroke, hoping the next one would result in her fingers touching the wall. Two more. Three max.

There was a splash beside her followed by a wake. She pulled hard and touched the wall.

A second behind Kevin.

Gasping for breath, she hung on to the side with one hand and wiped chlorine from her eyes with the other. Kevin's chest was heaving as fast as her own. He was inhaling, exhaling, lips white with exertion.

But still, she didn't miss his smile of victory, the glint in his you-didn't-think-I-could-do-it-did-you? eyes.

"Let me guess," she said between gasps. "Besides choir, you were on the swim team?"

"The first couple years. Then I got too busy. It's been a long time since. . . ." He eyed her steadily, his words trailing off.

For some reason, she didn't think he was talking about swimming anymore, which did nothing to slow her heart rate.

Michelle pushed off the wall and floated on her back, keeping her ears below water, listening to the muted sounds of her own labored breathing. She tried to relax, but the race was no longer the cause for her discomfort. Kevin was an interesting, multidimensional man. Okay. Sexy. Not a model-perfect specimen, but a man with depth, a passion seething right below the surface. She'd heard it earlier when he sang, and seen it these past few minutes in the way he attacked the lane. It wasn't just the competition that pushed him. She sensed something far deeper in this man—and the observation attracted and alarmed her at the same time.

She heard a splash and lifted her head in time to see his lean torso clear the water and amble over to his towel.

It was only Tuesday. How could she make it to Saturday without succumbing to this growing fantasy? As Kevin had started to say earlier, it had been a long time since. . . .

She swam to the side of the pool nearest her cover and, giving her suit a few last-second modesty tugs, used the steps and left the water.

Kevin wiped his face, then eyed Michelle standing by the ladder as she tightened the sash on her thin white cover-up. Within seconds, the moisture of her suit penetrated the outer fabric and her puckered nipples were clearly visible.

He groaned inwardly, feeling a tightness in his trunks. He hadn't thought it possible he'd experience such feelings again. Maybe it was merely lust. God knew he was overdue for a little action. But what bothered him was that he liked this woman and he wanted to know what made her tick. He'd always prided himself on being able to see past people's masks. Now he wondered what some man had done to Michelle to leave her so defensive and wary, so competitive and conflicted.

When he regained control of his traitorous body, he walked over to her, curious what persona she'd display next.

"What shall we do now?" he asked, a smile quirking his lips.

"We?" Her gaze darted back and forth. She picked up her beach bag and looked past him. "I don't know about you, but I want to get out of the sun, put on some dry clothes and maybe do a little shopping."

There was no invitation to join her. He took the hint with a mix of relief and disappointment. "Maybe I'll catch up on some reading back in my room, take a little nap." She didn't move. Had he misread her? Had she been expecting another response?

Women! Would he ever understand them?

"What if I pick you up at your room about seven and we take a walk before dinner?" He watched her indiscernible expression.

Then, slanting a questioning glance in his direction, she asked, "And exactly how do you plan to do that when you don't know my room number? Or do you?"

There was that suspicious mind of hers again. "I thought I'd walk you to your room now so I'd know where to go later. If that's okay with you." He could almost hear her thoughts—*What devious plan does he have in mind now?* Did she actually think he'd force his way into her room and attack her?

She nodded her head and hooked his arm. "Okay. Right this way."

Like he said, he knew a lot about women.

She lead him down the stairs, then aft along the Viking Deck hallway. She stopped at an outside stateroom at the far end and slipped her key into the lock. The door swung open, sun spilling through twin portholes. She spun around in the doorway and he nearly ran into her.

Kevin braced his hands on the doorjamb and peered beyond her, doing his best to ignore the proximity of her body to his. "Much nicer room than mine. There weren't any outsides left when I called." She didn't budge. He wasn't being invited in, but he noticed she didn't back away from him, either. He could feel her breath on his chest where his shirt hung open. He should turn and leave, keep it simple. But his feet felt like blocks of concrete.

In barely a whisper he said, "The bagpipes...they were..."

She lifted her chin and looked at him. "Very special," she finished, looking as nervous as he felt.

His gaze settled on her slightly parted lips. Like a magnet, they drew him closer, his mouth meeting hers as if it had a will of its own. She didn't push him away, but greeted him warmly, resting her hands on his hips.

Suddenly he pushed off the door, putting space between them. "Michelle. I, uh, I don't know what—" His voice caught in his throat and he couldn't meet her eyes.

"I'll see you at seven," she said hastily, her words running together. Then he heard the door close between them and he braved a glance at the threshold.

Had he lost control of his senses? What was he doing? He stared at the closed door another moment, then turned and walked away.


Michelle leaned against the door and held her breath until she heard his footsteps retreating. Then she let out a long sigh. She fingered her lips, heart still pounding. It was just one chaste little kiss. No tongues doing the tango. No heavy breathing. But her legs were trembling worse than she could remember them doing when she'd been an inexperienced teenager so many years ago.

She stumbled to the bed and sat down. Resting her elbows on her knees, she stared at the carpet between her feet.

"Whew..." She exhaled again, trying to slow her rapid pulse. "What's come over you, Purdue?" This fantasy-face thing was getting out of control.

She flopped back on the bed spread-eagled, a slow smile curving her lips.

Two consenting adults. Why not?

She sat up with a jolt. Sexually transmitted disease. That was why not. A blur of safe-sex commercials played in her mind's eye.

Condoms.

Ugh.

Could she actually go into a store and buy one?

One? That wouldn't do. But how did they come packaged, anyway? Three? Six? A dozen? A gross?

There was only one way to find out.

She changed quickly into shorts and a T-shirt and snatched her change purse off the dresser. Taking the stairs at a quick pace, she found what looked like a general store two flights up. She glanced nervously about as she stepped inside and caught her breath. She picked up a bestseller and read the jacket before strolling over to the personal needs section.

There she spotted the object of her search.

Holy Moses! Lubricated, ribbed, different sizes. How was a person to know size? She looked around to be sure no one was watching. Heaven forbid anyone thought she had sex, or was planning to. A soft chuckle emerged from the back of her throat.

Was she planning to have sex? Maybe. Well, just in case.

Michelle studied the selection in earnest, an unexpected excitement dancing through her. She eliminated the lubricated ones, already certain that wouldn't be a problem. The ribbed sounded a little erotic. As for size, she stuck with regular, pushing aside thoughts of how tight it might fit.

Michelle shook her head, grabbed a package of three, gathered her wits and proceeded quickly to the cashier. Her purchase safely bagged, she turned to leave.

She came to an abrupt stop.

"Michelle!" Kevin reached her with three long strides.

*Oh, God.* Had he seen? She eyed him cautiously, looking for signs of awareness. He didn't seem shocked or annoyed. If anything, he appeared a little ruffled at seeing her.

"I...I needed a new book," he stammered, shifting his gaze to the rack behind her. Then he looked down at the bag in her hand. "I see you started your shopping. Didn't waste much time." He smiled distractedly.

"This?" She held up the bag. "Toothpaste. Ran out of toothpaste." She forced a smile and headed for the door, calling over her shoulder. "See you at seven."

"You bet," he said to her back.

When she'd cleared the exit, Kevin strolled over to the personal-needs area and stopped in front of the display.

What the hell? Fluorescent? It'd been a long time, but he didn't think he'd have to glow in the dark to find it.

Looking right and left one last time, he grabbed a couple more conservative packets, snatched up the latest Michael Crichton paperback, paid for everything in a flurry and left the store.

# Five

Michelle bent at the waist and threw her hair forward, brushing vigorously from the nape of her neck to the blunt-cut ends. She'd decided to leave it down and loose tonight. No bobby pins, rubber bands or elaborate do. Clean and simple. Easier if...

*Damn.* She was obsessing again. This wasn't one of her romance novels. Kevin wasn't going to come swooping in and carry her to bed. She stood up and flung her hair back, noticing a few more strands of gold mixed with the copper. The past few days in the sun had done more than lighten her hair. It must have fried her brain. The light tap on the door made her jump. She glanced at her watch: seven on the nose.

"Okay, Purdue," she whispered. "Calm down. Act normal."

She straightened her shoulders, lifted her chin and opened the door, this time stepping back for Kevin to enter. Instantly she questioned her motives. Why hadn't she joined him in the hall? Now what?

Kevin moved slowly and silently to the portholes and gazed out. Michelle stood behind him, admiring the tailored fit of his slacks on his perfectly rounded backside just as he turned to face her. She was standing too close, but she didn't move. His dark eyes held her captive, trailing leisurely down her body and back to her face. His hands cupped her bare shoulders and she shivered at his tender touch. He was staring at her mouth again. Involuntarily she licked her lips, realizing the invitation it evoked.

She had to stop reading those books. She had to...she had to...

His mouth met hers gently and she lost all train of thought. His arms circled her back, his fingers spreading heat up and down her spine. The kiss deepened, his tongue moving slowly on hers, moist and trusting. In her mind she heard the bagpipes and his pure tenor voice, and again her legs began to shake, her knees about to buckle.

In one graceful move, Kevin picked her up and laid her on the double bed, sliding onto his side beside her, nibbling at her neck and shoulder. Slivers of light danced behind her closed lids as she enjoyed his every move. When his hand slid down her shoulder to her breast, she groaned aloud. Already she could feel moisture preparing the way for him.

She was glad he didn't speak. She didn't want to discuss it first. She didn't want to risk his saying anything that might change her mind.

Patiently, in a rhythm all his own, he undressed her, studying each new strip of exposed flesh as though she were a work of art. Surprisingly, she felt no shame or embarrassment. And when she was naked, she began removing his clothes at the same erotic pace.

When his boxers hit the floor, he rolled onto her and gazed deep into her eyes, with a look of caring far greater than passion, a look that brought tears to her eyes and a lump to her throat. This time, when his mouth met hers, their lips were hot and moist, the kiss more urgent. Her breathing escalated as he pressed his full arousal against her belly. Soon he would be inside her, filling a space too long neglected. Soon he...

*Yikes.* Soon she'd be having unprotected sex.

It was in the nightstand drawer. Still kissing him, she stretched one arm along the sheet as far as she could reach. She could feel the edge of the bed, but not the drawer. She shifted slightly beneath him and tried again. His mouth left hers and claimed her breast, suckling there a moment while his firmness pressed between her legs.

She had to get to the drawer. But how could she explain being so prepared? Just this afternoon she'd convinced him she wasn't on the make. Suddenly she whips out a foil packet? She groaned again as he pulled her to him, holding her tight.

She could feel his velvety tip against her. More than anything, she wanted to spread her legs and take him into her.

But suddenly he spoke between gritted teeth. "Don't... move." His breathing was jagged, much like her own. He straightened his arms on either side of her and stared at his pants on the floor. Then his eyes rolled to the ceiling and she felt spasms shudder through him.

"Damn." He avoided eye contact and lowered himself to her once again.

She felt the telltale warm liquid on her inner thighs and his hot breath against her cheek.

"I'm sorry, Michelle. It's been so long, I—"

"Shhh." She kissed his cheek and tightened her arms around his back. As much as her body screamed for more, her mind began taking over. The problem had been solved, albeit not very satisfactorily, but certainly more safely.

Kevin rolled on his side and eyed her sheepishly, his hand stroking her arm lovingly. "I guess I'm out of practice."

Michelle rolled toward him and met his gray gaze. "It's okay. Really."

Still breathing heavily, he flopped on his back and stared at the ceiling.

Michelle rolled on her stomach and prayed the blood would return to her head. Soon. Kevin said nothing for the longest time. Then suddenly she felt his gaze on the side of her face. She turned in time to see a smile working its way to his eyes.

"Was it good for you?" A self-deprecating chuckle passed his lips.

Michelle scooted higher on the bed until her hair touched the wall-mounted headboard. In a frustrated gesture that didn't seem forced, she began banging her head against the padded frame. "Oh, yeah. Terrific." When she stopped, she looked over her shoulder. He wasn't smiling. He might have thought she was serious if she hadn't started to laugh. Then he grabbed her around the waist and wrestled her to him, his own laughter warming her shoulder.

"Remember when we first met?" he asked, cradling her in his arms.

"How could I forget?"

"Well . . . it wasn't the greatest beginning." He looked down at her tenderly, his eyes full of promise. "But the second time was pretty special. Wouldn't you agree?"

She didn't answer. She hoped her smile told him she understood. Yes, there would be a second time. And if she read things right, a third and fourth, and who knew how many more? As if reading her mind, he began nibbling at her ear.

She pushed him back harder than she intended. "Wait!"

He sat up with a start and stared at her.

"Yes . . . I mean . . ." She sat up, too, and pulled the sheet to her chest. "We need to talk first." Her gaze darted from the sheet to the dresser drawer and back. If this was loving in the nineties, they could keep it. How was a person supposed to discuss history and safe sex without killing the mood?

Kevin stirred on the bed and she watched him reach for his pants on the floor. Was he getting dressed and leaving? Had she blown it already? But he didn't make a move to put the pants on. Instead, he held them in his hands, looking for all the world as if he wanted to say something but didn't know where to begin.

Michelle took a deep breath, then blurted out, "I was married for nearly ten years and I've been divorced for three. I haven't been with anyone since my ex." There. For what it was worth, she'd said it. Now it was his turn.

"Jessica and I were married for over twelve years." He lowered his eyes along with his voice. "She . . . well, we've been divorced almost four years. There's been no one since for me, either."

Michelle could hear something in his voice and she wanted to press for details, but something warned her to let it alone. Her divorce hadn't been exactly amicable, but she sensed his was a more painful subject. Did he still love this Jessica? Something resembling jealousy made her shiver.

Kevin reached for her hand and she jumped. He looked deep into her eyes, waiting several seconds before he spoke. "I haven't wanted to . . . until now."

She squeezed his hand, relieved and excited. "Neither have I."

A smile returned to his lips and she smiled back. Then she remembered the rest of her task. She released his hand and rolled quickly to the nightstand. Behind her she heard him rifling through his pants. She spoke before turning back to him. "Look, I know this probably looks presumptuous as hell, but when I was at the store this afternoon . . ." She turned back to him and stopped.

He held up a foil packet and finished her sentence. ". . . I bought some of these."

They eyed each other's purchases for a second, then burst into laughter.

"What kind did you get?" she asked, scooting closer.

"Your basic lubricated kind." He tossed the packet in her lap.

She tossed him hers. She almost said, "If you had waited a couple more seconds, you would've discovered we didn't need the lubricant." But she bit back what would have sounded like a complaint and instead said, "I was a little more creative. Note the 'ribbed.'"

The laughter continued, but suddenly it sounded more strained, embarrassment rearing its awkward head. Michelle glanced at the clock and let out a loud breath. It was after eight. Dinner was at eight-thirty.

"Did you hear my stomach growling?" Kevin asked.

"Is that what all that noise was about!"

His smile was devilish with a promise of more to come. He picked up the foil packets and placed them on the nightstand, giving them a stay-put pat. "Take your clothes and use the bathroom. I won't peek."

"My, but you're bossy." How long could she cover her shyness with playful repartee?

"You can dress here if you'd like . . . and I'll watch." He leaned back and locked his hands behind his head.

"Okay. You win. Turn around." When he had, she gathered her things and made a dash for the bathroom.

"Toss out a towel, would you please?" Kevin called after her.

She stuck out her arm and did as he asked, only to hear swearing a moment later.

"Now what?" Michelle asked through the closed door.

"Oh, nothing. I always wash from a bucket of melting ice."

Michelle laughed from the other side of the door, picturing him hopping about the room. Could this possibly be the same uptight guy she'd shared an agonizing dinner with only last Saturday? Boy, had she been wrong. A singer, a romantic, a sense of humor . . .

And a body ready to remember all the right moves.

His, too.

She freshened her lipstick and took one last appraising look. No lines on the forehead and a new brightness in her eyes.

This should prove an interesting night.


The sisters were already engaged in lively chatter with Mark and Kathy when Kevin pulled out Michelle's chair and they joined the table.

Millie stopped in midsentence and eyed them curiously. Kevin swallowed a silent oath. Discretion had never been a game he played well, but if he'd been thinking more clearly, he'd have let Michelle come alone and sauntered in later by himself. Then again, did it matter? The widows had been playing matchmakers since day one. Why not give them a little satisfaction?

He looked at Michelle who was taking her time opening her napkin on her lap, averting her eyes. He wished they'd discussed a plan first, but oh, well . . .

Kevin straightened in his chair and smiled broadly. "We had a terrific day. How was yours?" Out of the corner of his eye he saw Michelle's head pop up. Hazel and Millie exchanged a befuddled, openmouthed stare, but quickly recovered.

"Never mind about St. Martin," Millie started breathlessly. "It can wait. Tell us about your day." She winked at her sister who rolled her eyes.

Kevin looked at Michelle. She shot him a you-got-us-into-this-you-get-us-out kind of smile.

"Well, we swam a little, read some, went shopping." He risked a mischievous glance at Michelle who seemed to be swallowing a private joke along with her iced tea. She sat the glass down and eyed him coyly.

"Tell them about the best part," she began.

Kevin raised an eyebrow and he felt a not-too-gentle kick under the table.

With eyes widening she glared at him. "You know... the bagpipes."

"Ah, yes. The bagpipes." He met her stare evenly, until the corners of her mouth started to quiver. He pressed his thigh against hers under the table as he turned to the group and told the story. It was hard to concentrate on the details with Michelle's hand clutching his knee, but somehow he muddled through.

"Oh, I'm so sorry we missed that," Hazel said. "Millie and I have enjoyed that song in church for years. It's probably our favorite, wouldn't you say, sis?"

"Oh, my, yes. I don't think there's another song written that's as moving as 'Amazing Grace.' No matter how many times I hear it I cry." Millie sniffed. "Just thinking about it gets me all choked up." She dabbed daintily with her handkerchief, then brightened abruptly. "So you two shared this moment together? I mean, were you actually standing side by side when it happened?"

"Yes." Michelle and Kevin answered in unison, neither daring a sideways glance.

"Ah, that explains it," Millie said.

"Explains what?" the new groom asked. Kathy elbowed him as if to say "You know very well what."

Millie answered Mark's question anyway. "Why, they seem more relaxed with each other. Sis and I were worried—"

"Millie! Really!" Hazel butted in. "Why don't we tell them about St. Martin?" Hazel's tone of voice and pursed lips left Millie shaking her head in frustration, but she followed her sister's suggestion and began telling their tale. Soon the newlyweds joined in and stories of the island continued throughout dinner.

Kevin picked at his white fish, surprised at his lack of appetite. Though Michelle's hand was now busy with her fork, her thigh remained close to his—a simple act that obliterated all meaningful dialogue. Fortunately, he wasn't called on to speak. A nod or smile here and there sufficed.

As the conversation wound down and the last of the plates were cleared from the table, Mark covered a yawn with his tanned fingers. "Must be all the fresh air. I'm ready for bed." He wrapped an arm around his wife's shoulder and pulled her closer. "How 'bout you, sweetheart?"

Kathy met his gaze briefly, then stared at her lap. "I guess I'm sorta tired, too."

Mark shot out of his chair with renewed energy and held out his hand to his blushing bride. "See everyone tomorrow. Good night."

Kevin noticed the silent exchange in the pair's eyes as they made their hasty departure. Was it only last Saturday that he'd thought they were naive children? They might be young, but he thought they were on to something. Something that he felt far less critical of than he had in years.

Hazel placed her cold hand on his and he jumped.

"Are we going dancing tonight, Kevin?" she began. Suddenly she let out a sharp "Ouch!" and withdrew her hand.

"Poor Hazel." Millie shook her head and almost pulled off a sympathetic expression. "Those old legs aren't what they used to be, are they, dear?"

Hazel rubbed her leg under the table and shot her sister a look of loathing. "They're not as old as yours, dear." She leaned sarcastically on the endearment.

Millie gave her a playful wave as she rose from her chair. "Well, we've had enough for one day. Hope we run into you

two tomorrow." She waited at the end of the table for her tottering sister. "Say good-night, Hazel."

The woman patted Kevin and Michelle on their shoulders as
she limped past them. Then she gave them an impish smile.
"Good night, Hazel."

Kevin watched the matched set elbowing each other as they
moved away and he began to chuckle. When he turned back,
Michelle covered a yawn with the back of her hand. They eyed
each other a moment and then laughed aloud.

"Too subtle?" Michelle asked.

"Too tired?" Kevin shot back.

"What do you think?"

They were still laughing as they left the dining room and
double-timed the stairs, hand in hand.

# Six

___

Wednesday morning, Michelle felt the warm sun on her cheek and a protective hand on her bare backside. She opened one eye cautiously. Inches from her nose was Kevin's restful face. Gone were the stress lines on his forehead and the deep furrow between his thick brows. She listened to his soft breathing and watched his chest rise and fall.

When her gaze traveled back to his stubbled face, she noticed the corners of his mouth beginning a teasing turn upward. She met his sleepy gray eyes with a suggestive smile. "Good morning," she whispered.

He didn't answer, but brushed a kiss atop her hair and pulled her to him. Either he was glad to see her or nature called. She decided not to ask, luxuriating in his warm embrace.

"Did you notice the time?" Kevin asked in a husky voice.

Time? What was time? Michelle kissed his neck and mumbled, "Uh-huh."

"If we hurry, we can still do it."

She flopped on her back and stared wide-eyed at the clock. *Damn!*

"Want to skip it?" Kevin asked, propping himself up on his elbows.

"Do you?" she asked, uncertain.

"I have mixed feelings."

"Me too."

"But if we don't, we might regret it later." He was eyeing her with that playful and endearing look of his.

"A part of me hates to say it, but you're probably right." She heaved a big sigh. "Okay. Together, on the count of three."

He nodded his head and called out the numbers with her.

"One. Two. Three."

They both sprang from the bed on opposite sides. Kevin hurriedly pulled on his boxers and slacks. Michelle made a dash for the bathroom.

He spoke to her back. "I'll go to my room . . . shower and change. Whoever gets down there first save a place in line."

"Right," Michelle shouted over the water already spewing from the faucet. "Wear swim trunks underneath . . . just in case."

Seconds later, she stepped under the spray and shivered as the cold pelted her warm skin. She lathered quickly and swore under her breath. She had no one to blame but herself. She was the one who had suggested they get off at St. Thomas this morning. Another of her bright ideas.

She dried hurriedly and shimmied into her bikini bottoms, hooking the top a moment later. She found a lightweight gauzy sundress in the closet. It was sea-mist green and wrapped in the front with a sash. She slipped it on along with her most comfortable leather sandals. Her hair was still wet, but there wasn't time to fuss. She brushed it away from her face, pulling it high on her head and securing it with a green fabric twister. Stepping away from the mirror, she glanced at the clock near the bed. It would have to do. The handwoven bag in the corner caught her attention. She spilled its contents onto the floor, found her wallet, sunscreen and a clean towel, then headed for the door.

Walking as fast as her legs would carry her, she shoved the few items into the bag and threw it over her shoulder.

She spotted Kevin near the front of the line as she rounded the last corner. Slowing her pace, she blew out a long breath. They hadn't missed the early tender, after all. Kevin turned and waved her over, his chestnut hair still wet, shining in the morning sun. Her heart raced as she sauntered toward him. In spite of other desires, she was glad they were going ashore. It was a beautiful day. Not a cloud marred the perfect blue sky and a faint breeze made the hot sun comfortable on her bare arms and legs.

She took his extended hand and together they boarded the smaller boat, seconds before it revved its engines and headed for shore. They leaned on the railing in companionable silence, squawking gulls circling overhead, as the transport closed the distance to St. Thomas.

Finally, the picturesque city of Charlotte Amalie, resplendent with its dazzling white and brilliant pastel buildings, came alive behind the crowded waterfront. Kevin squeezed her hand, and excitement surged through her.

An historic Caribbean island, and a handsome and caring man to share it with. It couldn't get better than this.

Could it? She brushed the question aside.

They stepped ashore, hand in hand and headed for Tolbod Gade and the Grand Hotel. But before they'd gone a few yards, Michelle swayed and stumbled into Kevin's side.

"Excuse me," she said, feeling a little dizzy.

Kevin wrapped his arm around her waist and held her steady. "Sea legs," he said, giving her a squeeze. "Just when you get them, you don't want them. It'll pass." He winked at her. "But I'd better hang on to you tight in the meantime."

Michelle studied the warm gray eyes that gazed down at her so tenderly and something lurched in the area of her heart. She released his hold and sat on a bench behind them.

Her legs felt better, but her heart didn't. It was one thing to give in to a shipboard romance, to give herself permission to lust after someone as good-looking and kind as Kevin. But to feel more was dangerous. It would be difficult enough to walk away come Saturday. Caring more would only make it harder.

Kevin sat beside her looking concerned. "Are you okay?"

She pulled herself out of her private reverie and nodded. "Still want to rent a car and go exploring?" she asked on a sigh.

"Sure," he started, then paused. "If you're up to it."

"Coffee and a bagel and I'll be raring to go." She forced a lightness into her voice she didn't feel.

"A bagel?" He shook his head and laughed. "You stay put. I'll get a car before they're all gone. Then we'll see if we can find you a bagel."

His hand traveled back and forth just above her knee and her thoughts returned to last night, the feel of him so close...

"Any preference?" he asked, pushing off the bench.

Preference? Lips parted slightly, she stared at him a moment before she realized what he meant. "Oh. You mean car?"

He chuckled easily. "No. Onion or cinnamon and raisin. You sure you're okay?"

She stood abruptly, her legs still feeling like spaghetti. "Positive. In fact, why don't I go up to the Grand Hotel where there's a visitors' guide and restaurant? I'll get us a map and something to go while you get the car." She saw a red open-air Jeep pass by and pointed to it. "See if they have any of those left." Slowly she turned away from him and began walking toward town, trying her best not to look like a drunken sailor.

Hands on hips, Kevin watched Michelle snake her way down the road. Now what was that all about? he wondered, turning back for the car-rental place he'd spotted near the docks. She'd looked at him as if she were seeing him for the first time.

And she hadn't looked too pleased with what she saw.

Was she sorry she'd committed to spending the day with him? He weaved his way through throngs of tourists heading in the opposite direction, his thoughts on the past twelve hours.

Everything had felt so perfect. Maybe too perfect. It was hard to believe he'd known this woman only since Saturday. He got in line at the car-rental booth, a dark mood stealing his newfound happiness.

How was he going to feel when it was time to say goodbye?

Fifteen minutes later, Kevin signed the paperwork for a red Jeep, jumped behind the wheel and gripped the steering wheel. Slowly, he scanned the interior, then tipped his head back. It'd been years since he'd been in a convertible, and he'd never driven a Jeep. The day had all the potential for a memorable one.

If he didn't screw it up with maudlin thoughts.

He turned the key in the ignition and cupped the gearshift, deciding a change in attitude was in order.

Moist, hot air lifted the hair off his forehead as he neared the main street of Norre Gade. The narrow streets already teamed with excited tourists swarming like ants in the historic shopping district. Behind him was the harbor flanked by warehouses. Images of marauding pirates and fabled treasures did nothing to slow his racing pulse. He couldn't remember the last time he'd felt so alive. He saw a sign pointing east to Bluebeard's Castle and almost missed the Grand Hotel on his right. It was a splendid example of nineteenth-century architecture. He tried focusing on the details of its exterior instead of the woman inside, but that proved impossible.

He found a parking spot and started up the steps as Michelle bounded toward him, her ponytail swinging behind her, her excitement unbridled. She handed him both covered cups of coffee and retrieved the booklet sticking out of her shoulder bag.

"You won't believe all there is to do." She started flipping through pages.

Kevin watched with amusement, knowing whatever they did would be interesting, to put it mildly. If he could take his eyes off her for more than fleeting moments, maybe he'd even see some of this island.

"Oh, Kevin!" She brushed by him and raced to the unoccupied red Jeep a few car lengths away. He followed close behind. "Is this ours?"

She looked like a little girl on Christmas morning. If his hands weren't occupied with coffee, he'd have snatched her up in his arms. "It's what you ordered," he said, controlling his own excitement.

She hopped into the passenger seat and explored the interior while he walked around and joined her. "Where shall we begin?"

"Wherever you think they sell bagels." He couldn't keep the chuckle out of his voice.

"No need." She opened her bag and handed him a warm slice of banana bread. "Much better, don't you think?" She sniffed at her own piece, then took a bite, not waiting for his response. "Let's see," she began, thumbing through the booklet until something caught her eye. "Ooh. Look at the view from here!" She turned the page in his direction and showed him Mountain Top, the highest point on the island. "Do you think we can find this place?"

"How difficult can it be? If I remember the brochure from the ship, this whole island is only thirteen miles long and three miles wide. Just point me in the right direction."

"It says here to follow the banana signs."

"Banana signs?"

Michelle read from the glossy page. "The banana daiquiris served here are legendary. They serve more than two hundred and fifty thousand of them every year."

"I think I can handle that."

"Then I'd better plan to drive back." She shot him an impish grin, then turned her attention to the passing scenery.

Kevin took a long swallow of coffee, wondering if Michelle would allow herself one little daiquiri, or if her no-alcohol policy was inflexible. He secured the half-full cup between his legs and maneuvered the vehicle through the narrow streets and away from the bustling city. Whether she ever had a drink or not wasn't his concern, he lectured himself. Still, he couldn't help but wonder about the rest of that story. There was usually a reason when someone didn't drink a drop.

They passed Bluebeard's Castle, built on a low hill overlooking the harbor, and Michelle filled him in on the legendary pirate who had lived there during the seventeenth century. The story went that he had had seven wives, one of whom poisoned the other six and was saved from the gallows by her husband at the eleventh hour.

Kevin honked at a friendly herd of goats who ambled along in front of them, not seeming to mind human intruders. Michelle laughed and reached out to pet one as they inched by. Kevin moved forward slowly, stealing glances at the passenger seat at every opportunity. As much as he loved the beauty of everything that surrounded them, he loved watching her enjoy herself more. He finished his coffee, crumpled the cup and deposited it under the seat, all the time fighting the need to know more about this woman beside him.

They drove on in silence, stirring an occasional cloud of dust when they hit a bumpy spot. The speed limit said thirty-five miles per hour, but he never got out of first gear as they climbed to fifteen hundred feet above sea level. A couple stray cows later, they reached Mountain Top and found a parking spot near an observation deck.

Michelle ran from the Jeep, ponytail swinging behind her, loose tendrils blowing in the wind. She didn't stop until she reached the railing. Kevin approached slowly, looking past her at the unparalleled view of Magens Bay, but his gaze returned quickly to the childlike wonder that filled Michelle's face. Was it the romantic setting or this woman that sent chills up and down his damp shirt? Whichever, he had to remember that both would be gone come Saturday.

Without a sideways glance, Michelle wrapped her arm around his waist and pulled him closer. "Have you ever seen anything more beautiful?"

Kevin looked down at her and smiled. "No. Never."

"Oh, look!" She pointed, seeming unaware of the lump he'd just swallowed. "Over there. That island must be St. John. The smaller ones have to be Tortola and Virgin Gorda. Do you know which is..." Finally she met his gaze and let the question die on her lips.

He turned her toward him and trailed his hands down her warm, bare arms, feeling the telltale swelling in his groin. He stared at her inviting lips, remembering the taste and feel of them shortly before dawn. Abruptly he stiffened his arms and held her away from him, slowing his pulse before he spoke.

"I have an idea." He winked at her playfully.

"I bet you do," she said, eyeing him from the side of her face.

"You said something about a cafeteria up here. Let's have them pack us a couple salads and sandwiches. One of the gift shops must sell picnic blankets."

"I'll get the food. You find the blanket." She hopped on both feet in front of him, a smile creasing her tanned face.

"Meet you back here?" he asked.

"Right," she called over her shoulder, already several yards down the trail.

They sat cross-legged on two banana-patterned beach towels overlapped in the middle and stared at what *National Geographic* named one of the world's ten most beautiful beaches. What a job *that* must be, Michelle thought—traveling the world and rating beaches. She wondered if the critics traveled alone or with loved ones. With Kevin, she wondered if she could be objective. They would all seem special.

She reached for the bag of food, reminding herself this was one of life's ports of call. Nothing permanent. Enjoy the moment. That's all there is or ever will be.

She busied herself rooting around in the bag, afraid to meet Kevin's eyes. He'd know she wanted more, and that had never been part of the deal. "Hungry yet? Or how about an infamous Banana Daiquiri?" She pulled out a large insulated covered mug and gave it a shake. There was a second one in the bag, sans rum, in a different color. There was a question in his eyes and she could guess what it was, but she offered no explanation.

"I think I'd rather just sit here and soak up the sights." He lifted his face to the sun, then slowly scanned the horizon. "It truly is magnificent, isn't it?"

Michelle studied his handsome and relaxed profile. "Yes. It is." Why wasn't there a man like this at home? She didn't think it was merely the setting, though it would be difficult to top this one. No. It was the man himself that made this time so perfect. She looked at his fingers splayed on the towel, supporting his weight behind him. What did he really do for a living? Sitting here, feeling the rippled sand beneath her bottom, she felt something else—the tender, swollen parts of her. The parts that his gentle yet sure fingers stroked and caressed. This was not a man who worked with two-by-fours and plywood. She wished, at least for today, that they could drop the pretenses.

More than anything, she wished he would talk about himself—where he lived, what he did, and how he felt. About her.

She returned the insulated cup to the bag and burrowed a spot in the sand next to her to keep the bottom cool, covering the top with the towel from her room. Now she had to work on keeping herself cool. This current line of thinking was dangerous, destined for disappointment. If Kevin wanted to share his life story, he would have by now. She had to appreciate what she had—the here and now.

Brushing the sand off her hands, she stood and walked to the water's edge. It was warm, the bottom clean and inviting. She waded out, small waves breaking against her calves. *Live for the moment.* Like a mantra, she kept repeating it in her head. *Live for the moment.*

Before she was thigh-deep, Kevin intertwined his fingers in hers. Together they bobbed and staggered their way deeper until a wave caught Michelle under the chin and they submerged themselves completely.

She wondered what he was thinking. Words weren't necessary, she kept telling herself. She knew everything she needed to know about Kevin. He was kind, loving, gentle and good.

Out of bed, too.

She laughed aloud and swallowed a mouthful of salt. When she started coughing, Kevin pulled her to him, pressing the length of himself against her and slapping her back. She half coughed, half laughed into his chest. This proximity wasn't helping. Neither was his left hand, which had slid possessively between her swimsuit bottom and wet skin, pushing her tighter against his firmness. And here she'd thought he was acting paternal. She pushed away with one last cough, finding her footing a couple of yards to his side.

So he wanted to be playful, did he? She looked toward their towels, then at the boats far from shore. No one without binoculars could see them. With one deft flick of her thumb and forefinger, she unhooked her top and waved it high in the air, a chartreuse flag flying proud above her head. His slack jaw as he stared back at her was reward enough, but she couldn't help pushing a little further. "Your turn, cowboy."

"Cowboy?" He stood with arms akimbo, smirking. He was egging her on. She could see it in his eyes and stance.

"Yeah. Cowboy. The way you were bucking and riding last night, the name fits, don't you think?"

Even with his new layer of pink from the sun, she could have sworn he was blushing. "What's the matter? You chicken?"

He reached below the water and, hopping on one leg then the other, removed his trunks and held them up for her to see. "Okay, smarty-pants, your turn."

There was something in his eyes that said he'd won this little game. *Well, we'll see about that,* she thought. She shrugged out of her bottoms, balled both pieces in her hand and tossed them his way. They floated a few feet in front of him. Quickly he scooped them up and headed for shore.

"Why, you little devil," Michelle called after him.

He stopped where the water was waist-high and called back to her. "What's the matter? You chicken?"

She laughed heartily. "What's to be chicken about? You've already seen everything I've got."

His expression was one of victory. "That's true. But that guy behind you hasn't." He waded in, the white of his backside coming into view. He walked to their belongings and picked up the ship's towel before turning back to her, a smug smile plastered on his amused face.

No. She wasn't going to fall for that trick. She'd watched too many old westerns to know no one was pointing a gun to her back, forcing her to surrender. Just to be certain, she stood perfectly still, listening for splashes or voices nearby. Nothing.

*Live for the moment. Live for the moment.*

With head held high and a cocky grin, she took long strides and met him on the sand. He had slipped into his soggy trunks and was holding the damp towel in her direction.

"Want this one or a sandy banana?"

Michelle stood naked in front of him, her back to the water, feeling wicked and thoroughly entertained. "Neither. Think I'll let the sun do its job." She spread her legs, then bent at the waist and threw her ponytail forward, spraying him intentionally in the process. She giggled while squeezing the excess water from the tips of her hair. She took her time, taunting him, until she gazed out at the water from between her knees and saw the yellow raft. She let out a high-pitched squeal that to her own ears sounded like a caged monkey's, and then darted for cover behind Kevin. He held out the towel and she snatched it.

"Don't say I didn't warn you."

She kicked him behind one knee and he went down in the sand, turning and taking her with him as he fell. He rolled her onto her back and pinned her beneath him. "How much of a show do you want to give that guy?"

"I think he's had enough for one day, don't you?"

Cheek to cheek, they turned their heads to the gently rolling sea. A bald-headed man waved, his toothy smile gleaming from the distance before he paddled on.

"Satisfied?" she asked, trying to sound like a poor loser. Kevin's nose was an inch from hers.

"Not if we stay in this position much longer." Bracing his hands on either side of her, he stood and began to laugh.

"What?" she asked, clutching the sandy towel to her chest as she rose.

"Nothing." His laughter stopped and his face took on a surprised look. "I'm just having fun."

There was more he seemed to have on his mind, but he didn't say it. Instead, he sat on the banana towels and reached into the bag for his daiquiri.

If only Paul could see him now. He chuckled and took a hefty swig from the sweaty cup. All his friend had suggested was someplace warm with women in bikinis. He'd never believe this. Any of it.

Kevin watched Michelle kick low-breaking waves as she sauntered down the beach to the public rest room they'd spotted driving in. Her clothes were draped over one arm, the sandy towel over her shoulder. She'd said she needed to get the salt off, but he suspected she needed a little space, too. Or was that what he needed? If she'd stayed another five minutes he would have told her everything—what he did, where he lived. Probably about his divorce, too. What a way to ruin a perfect day. What woman wants to hear about an ex-wife?

But for some reason he wanted to tell Michelle. Except with his attorney and Paul, Kevin hadn't mentioned Jessica's name since the day she moved out, which probably wasn't the healthiest way to handle the problem, but it had seemed easier at the time. Now, after all these years, he wondered if Jessica hadn't hurt his ego more than his heart when she made her little announcement. *I'm pregnant...by one of my partners in the firm.* His opinion of lawyers had hit an all-time low that day. Before then he hadn't had a clue she'd been unfaithful, let alone pregnant. If he hadn't witnessed her morning sickness that day, how long would the charade have continued? Kevin finished his daiquiri in one long swallow.

It was a good thing Michelle had left when she did. There was no point in dumping all this old garbage on her. For what purpose? To draw her closer? He had a sinking feeling things had gone too far already.

How would he ever say goodbye?

# Seven

Thursday morning, Michelle and Kevin stood outside the ship's drugstore.

"You go in." She nudged him toward the door.

"Me? Why me?"

"Because it's the same clerk I bought them from just a few days ago."

"So?"

"So, what will he think?"

Kevin winked at her. "That you practice safe sex?"

"Practice? Is that what we've been doing?"

"Until we get it right," he whispered near her ear.

Michelle punched his arm. "Come on, please? You go. It's easier for guys."

"What feminist magazine did you read that in?"

She pouted and cocked her head, giving him her best pretty-please expression.

"Okay, okay. You win."

She pecked him on the cheek and darted off before he could change his mind. "I'll meet you by the pool," she called over her shoulder, not wanting to see the look on his face.

She practically skipped along the railing, happiness bursting through her skin. It was like nothing she'd felt since childhood. There was nothing childlike in the game they were playing. But there was nothing wrong with it, either.

It might have been only five days, but she felt as if she'd known Kevin forever. And not just his body. Though she couldn't deny it was an exciting part of what she felt. It was so much more. The feel of his arms around her, cocooning her from the emptiness she'd felt for so long, the smiles he brought to her lips. The laughs they shared. Often. Sometimes when they were making love—a new experience for her.

Kevin had her same quirky sense of humor—one she'd always thought was hers alone. Yet there was a deeper, tender side of him, too. Like when he'd sung to the bagpipes, or softly in her ear on the dance floor late last night after they returned from St. Thomas, and again this morning in the shower.

Michelle deposited their towels on a pair of chaise longues next to the pool facing the sun. She sat down, closed her eyes and tilted her head to the warm rays. Next to being inseminated, this trip was the best decision she'd ever made. And to think she'd only hoped to find a fantasy *face* for the father. Now she had a whole person to remember when the time came.

And the time would come. She was sure of it. Perhaps this wonderful week with Kevin had gotten her hopes up falsely, but she didn't think so. Unconsciously she circled her sun-warmed stomach with her palm, just as a shadow crossed her face.

"You can't be hungry already," Kevin said, gazing down at her. "After that huge breakfast you wolfed down?"

Michelle's hand stopped moving. "You're right. I'm stuffed. Just checking to see how many inches I've added this week." She smiled up at him, feeling a little deceptive and trying to hide it.

Kevin peeled off his T-shirt and stretched out alongside her. "I doubt you've gained any weight this week. Between the swimming and..." He eyed her tenderly and didn't finish the sentence.

"I think I'd like to relax and read a little before I beat you at laps." She was purposefully redirecting the conversation, doing her best to lighten the dark mood that had suddenly crept over her.

"Huh! That'll be the day." Kevin withdrew a newspaper from his bag of purchases and snapped it open with an air of self-confidence. "You haven't beat me yet. What makes you think today will be any different?"

She was glad he stuck his nose in the paper and didn't look her way. There was a sudden mist over her eyes that he surely would have noticed. She swallowed hard and said, "Shhh... I'm reading."

He read. She thought.

She turned pages not seeing a word. This week had been a miracle—hopefully in two ways. With any luck one was a reality. But what about Kevin? As successful as she'd been all week at denying the truth, she had feelings for this man that far transcended fantasy. She didn't know his last name, or what he did for a living, or where he lived. But she knew the man. Maybe better than she had any other.

Had it been so comfortable because there were no decisions to make? No commitment? Did the lack of those pressures make it seem easy and natural?

She put the book down and rolled onto her stomach, facing away from Kevin. Tomorrow afternoon there was a farewell picnic and the next day the cruise would end. They'd walk down that gangplank and out of each other's lives. Sure, she could ask him his last name and address. He might even agree to keep in touch. But how long would that last? Phone calls and letters would only add to the frustration of not seeing him. Besides, she had a demanding career and, hopefully, a baby on the way. The last thing she needed was a man complicating her life.

She swiped at a tear streaking down her temple. She'd known this would end before it started. But, damn, she hadn't thought it would be so painful.

Without a sideways glance at Kevin, she pushed off the chaise longue, shrugged out of her cover-up and moved to the deep end of the pool. She dived long and shallow, swimming half the distance of the pool underwater before her lungs begged for air.

When her head cleared the water she did the breaststroke to the far wall, then pushed off with a lazy backstroke.

The best thing for the blues was exercise, she reminded herself. There was no point in ruining what little time they had left. If tears had to come—and right now she was sure they would—then they'd have to wait until Kevin was gone. He wouldn't see her clinging, acting as if there should be more than he promised. If he wanted more, he would have said something by now. He'd had plenty of opportunity yesterday to talk about himself and end their little game, but he hadn't. She rolled over and increased her pace, telling herself it was for the best.

If she said it often enough, maybe she'd believe it.

Kevin dropped the paper on his lap and watched Michelle glide through the water. A heaviness weighed on his chest. After Jessica, he'd thought he'd never trust another woman enough to care as much as he did about Michelle. He certainly hadn't thought he'd feel the way he did now when this week began. He chuckled under his breath, remembering the first time he'd spotted her on deck, and how carefully he'd avoided her the next day. Who would have thunk...

His smile faded. Saturday was fast approaching. How would it end when they docked? A quick hug and peck on the cheek as he strode off? Maybe a carefree wave over his shoulder? He just couldn't picture it.

But he had better. Soon.

It was a calm and lazy Friday morning when the ship approached Great Stirrup Cay, Norwegian Cruise Line's own private island. Michelle scanned the faces of the crowd preparing to go ashore. She wasn't the only somber passenger. Others had that resigned demeanor about them, too, as if they were simply going through the motions—*Tell us where to go, what to do.... We know it's almost over and the real world is about to swallow us up come tomorrow.*

Kevin had begged off, saying he had some reading he had to catch up on—work-related, whatever that was. He'd suggested she go to the picnic and enjoy herself.

Already he was pulling away. Earlier, when he kissed her goodbye, he'd avoided her eyes. Michelle pulled a tissue from her shorts pocket and gave a good blow.

*Grow up, Purdue. You knew what you were getting into.*

"There you are!" Millie stretched out both arms as she and Hazel approached. "Are you and Kevin going to the picnic?"

Michelle averted her gaze. "I am." Why, she didn't know, but it beat standing around feeling sorry for herself.

"Not Kevin?" Hazel asked, sounding both surprised and disappointed.

"No. He's staying on the ship."

"Oh, dear. You two didn't have a spat, did you?" Millie rubbed Michelle's arm, comforting her over what she assumed was true.

Michelle expelled a long sigh, and with it her maudlin thoughts, and smiled. "No, not at all. He had some things he had to do. Mind if I tag along with you two today?"

The sisters brightened noticeably. "We'd love your company," Millie said, then looked to Hazel for confirmation.

"Oh, yes, yes. We'll have a delightful day," Hazel said, her blue head bobbing with excitement.

And so they did. The threesome strolled leisurely along paths, stopping to smell the hibiscus, Millie pinching a red one off and tucking it above Michelle's ear. They spotted birds and foliage, trying to beat each other with the names of each as if they were contestants on "Jeopardy." They talked of everything and nothing, finding a bench here and there to rest. When they joined the other travelers for the midday picnic, they sat together, still not tired of each other's company.

Michelle watched the pair nibble daintily on chicken wings and a warmth trickled through her. She couldn't remember feeling this way since her parents had died. She'd never had aunts, but she imagined this was how she'd have felt about them if she had. It was a pity she'd have to say goodbye to these wonderful ladies tomorrow, too.

But then, maybe she didn't. Kevin was one thing. They were another.

She decided a little probing couldn't hurt. "Are you two flying out of Miami Airport tomorrow?" she asked, trying to sound conversational rather than nosy.

Millie pouted before she answered. "Unfortunately, yes. We always hate for these things to end..."

"To say goodbye to new friends," Hazel finished for her.

Millie looked coyly at her sister, then pushed some potato salad around on her plate. "We noticed you and Kevin never mentioned your last names or where you were from...."

"Well, we—" Michelle began, but Hazel held up her hand, palm forward.

"It's okay, dear," she began. "You can't be too careful these days. Besides, we respect people's privacy, whatever the reasons."

"On the other hand," Millie jumped in, smiling expectantly, "if someone wants to tell us something, we're all ears."

Michelle laughed aloud. "You two." She shook her head and eyed them affectionately. "It's been fun getting to know you this week." She reached across the table and took one of their hands in each of hers, squeezing gently their frail little fingers. "I'm especially glad you let me join you today." She felt a catch in her throat.

"It's been our pleasure, Michelle," Millie said, her eyes misting over.

Hazel honked loudly into her ever-present hanky, and they all laughed heartily.

Millie was first to gain control. "Did you say you're leaving from Miami Airport, too?"

"No, I didn't."

The pair groaned in unison.

"But I am," Michelle finished, watching their frowns turn to smiles. "I have a late-morning flight to Detroit."

"Detroit!" Again they spoke at the same time. Then they looked at each other and smiled a knowing smile.

Hazel spoke first. "What do you know? We must be on the same plane."

Michelle saw the wheels turning behind Millie's scheming eyes and knew instantly that she hadn't seen the last of this pair, which was great, as far as she was concerned. Maybe she'd l this cruise with merely a fantasy father for her child, but there was no reason she couldn't have a couple aunts . . . or grand-mothers.

Millie dabbed at her mouth with her napkin, then set it aside with an air of something important to come. "We don't live in Detroit, dear. Do you?"

Michelle's disappointment was nearly palpable. "Yes. I do." She sipped iced tea and tried to mask her feelings.

"We live just across the Ohio state line . . . in Toledo," Hazel was quick to add.

Michelle sat her glass down and took in their smiling faces in a single glance. "That can't be much more than an hour or so drive." She knew they were waiting for her to make the first gesture. And she didn't disappoint them.

Hazel retrieved pens and paper from her handbag and they wrote names, addresses and phone numbers and exchanged them with newfound excitement.

"You wouldn't believe our Christmas card list," Hazel said, finding just the right place in her bag for the new information.

"Not that we always wait for Christmas, mind you," Millie added. "Since we're so close by, maybe we can get together sometime. We took lots of pictures. You and Kevin are in several." Millie stopped suddenly when Michelle looked away. "Did I say something wrong, dear?"

Michelle took her time answering, not sure how to explain. Finally, she decided the truth was best, but only the bare necessities. "Kevin and I don't know each other's last names or where the other lives. We don't plan to communicate once the cruise ends."

Millie held her steady gaze, questions obviously warring inside her head. But to her credit, she didn't pry.

"Your secret is safe with us, dear."

There was an awkward silence and Michelle was tempted to volunteer more, but with great restraint she lowered her gaze, drank more tea and waited for one of them to speak.

It didn't take long. The subject was dropped, replaced by more history of Great Stirrup Cay and how it had come to be

Michelle half listened, grateful for the distraction, but her thoughts drifted. She thought about the person who wouldn't be at the airport tomorrow. Or would he?

*Don't do this to yourself, Purdue.*

It had been a wonderful week, one that she would cherish always. She'd gained two new friends whom she would talk to from time to time. Her life was so much richer for having taken this vacation.

Then why did she feel as if someone had just cut through her chest and yanked out her heart?

Kevin gave up reading his journals in exchange for a little shopping, which in itself should have told him something was wrong. He hated shopping. But his office manager and Paul deserved gifts. They'd earned them, actually. Especially Paul, who had forced this vacation on him. No gift could ever match his friend's sage decision, but something special was in order.

He wandered into a duty-free shop and found himself staring at the jewelry counter. A heart-shaped aquamarine pendant on a delicate white-gold chain stared back at him. This definitely wouldn't look good on Paul. He chuckled under his breath. And it seemed too extravagant, too personal for his manager.

But it was perfect for Michelle.

He hesitated all of thirty seconds before he asked the clerk to wrap it for him, a smile tugging at the corners of his mouth as he thought of the perfect way to give it to Michelle. A way she couldn't refuse.

Finding something for Paul and his manager swallowed the remainder of the afternoon, just as he'd hoped it would, bridging the afternoon alone and the evening with Michelle.

Kevin knotted his tie and tightened it, feeling choked even before he finished. He'd sit next to Michelle at dinner for the last time. Maybe they'd dance a little afterward. For the last time. And then they'd stroll the decks to her room . . . and her bed. For the last time.

He squared his shoulders and inhaled deeply, his jaw muscles remaining clenched. The reflection in the mirror seemed foreign to him. The tanned man with less stress around the eyes also looked sadder. This cruise had brought him an inner peace he'd been lacking for years, but the price of peace was growing higher by the minute.

Kevin tore his gaze away from the mirror and left the room, his stride long and determined. Somehow, he'd get through this night.

But what about all the nights after this?

He had a second week booked at an oceanfront hotel. Once he got back to work things would get easier, but a week of solitude, staring at the same ocean shared with Michelle, sounded like slow torture.

The thought tore at his gut as he approached their table, her easy laugh with Millie and Hazel etching itself on his memory, along with her flowing red hair and bare, freckled brown shoulders, along with accumulated hours of so much more.


Michelle heard the last call for boarding and scanned the area one last time. She knew he wouldn't be there, but she let herself hope until the last possible second.

Slowly she turned and walked toward the gate, images of last night fresh and raw, too bittersweet. She could still smell his musky after-shave as he'd held her tight on the dance floor. Worse, she could still feel him inside her as she'd pretended to doze in his arms after.

They had talked about it and agreed. When she was asleep he would leave her. No goodbyes. No tears.

She handed her boarding pass to the stewardess and walked down the jetway, numb from a sleepless night and missing Kevin more than she thought she could bear.

# Eight

---

**W**ork had always been her refuge. A place in her mind where she could get lost for hours on end with nonpersonal, non-emotional tasks, tasks that yielded immediate gratification.

Michelle pushed away from the computer, rolled her neck and flexed her fingers. Yesiree, nothing like a couple of data base projects to absorb her days. And weeks. To keep her mind off the calendar.

And the cruise.

Kevin What's-His-Name. The contractor with the soft, slow hands.

Contractor, my eye. She fingered the pendant that hung from her neck—the one she'd found tucked in her suitcase when she unpacked after the cruise, the one she'd worn ever since.

No! She couldn't afford to drift back again. In time the memories would merge with the hundreds of novels she'd read. He'd become just another handsome hero, another romantic escape from harsh reality.

*Right.*

She slapped her knees with her palms and stood. Her coffee cup was empty and so was her well of energy. This past week had been the worst. She refilled her mug and leaned against the kitchen counter, feeling the familiar knot tightening in her chest. The calendar on the wall next to the phone loomed larger than life. She didn't have to look at it to know it was June 6 and she had just missed a second period. Still, no morning sickness or other telltale signs.

The test kit waited in the bathroom medicine cabinet. It would be simple enough to find out. But was she ready for bad news? She hadn't been last month at this time. The kit had sat on the counter for days until finally she put it away. She'd known that if she tested positive then, she might miscarry early. She still could, but waiting seemed easier than heartbreak. Hope and her goosedown pillow were the only things she clung to during the lonely hours of the night when Kevin's face haunted her, over and over, every time she closed her eyes, and even when she didn't.

Michelle slapped the mug on the counter and coffee sloshed over the side, leaving a puddle around it. She took a deep breath, exhaled slowly and marched to the bathroom before she could change her mind.

Seconds later she stood in front of the vanity, eyes closed, the narrow strip between her fingers. Her chest rose and fell faster, her emotions ready to burst through her skin. Moisture from her lashes brushed her cheeks. Slowly, cautiously, she opened her eyes and stared straight ahead, seeing nothing. She blinked hard, clearing her vision. Finally, she looked down to her shaking fingers. Stilling her right hand with her left, she blinked again and took a long, hard look.

Blue.

She drew the strip closer to her face. No doubt about it. It was blue. She lifted the box with the directions and double-checked.

"Yes!" She spun in a circle, dizzy with excitement. "Yes, yes, yes!!!"

She continued her dance down the hall to her bedroom, then dropped on her bed, spread-eagled. Tears ran down her temples wetting her hair, but her smile widened and quivered, a laugh bursting from her lips. She pulled her pillow over her chest and hugged it. "Thank you, God. Oh, thank you. You won't be sorry you trusted me on this one."

She sat up and swiped at her wet face with the backs of her hands. Who could she call? She wanted to tell someone. Oh, God! She couldn't believe it. She was going to be a mother.

With renewed energy, she ran to the kitchen and took the calendar off the wall and began calculating. Early January. She did it again and came up with the same answer. How would she get through Christmas, waiting for the most important present of her life? Maybe she'd arrive early. She? Or was it a he?

Her legs started to tremble, and she sat at the table, feeling like someone else. Some alien occupied her body; Michelle Purdue was somewhere else. She had never experienced this magical feeling. Was she awake? She wanted to laugh and cry, all at the same time.

She sprang to her feet and began pacing her small apartment. What should she do next? Certainly not work, not yet. She looked at the kitchen clock: almost noon. The doctor's office closed for lunch. Her fingers tripped over the numbers twice before she got it right. The familiar voice answered on the second ring, and Michelle exhaled to the ceiling.

"This is Michelle Purdue. Is this Kelly?"

"All day long," she said, an easy lilt in her friendly voice.

"Kelly, I need an appointment as soon as possible."

"Are you ill?" she asked, sounding sincerely concerned.

"No... Yes... I mean ... well, I think I'm pregnant."

"Ohhh ..." Kelly said, with an all-knowing tone, a smile evident in her youthful voice.

Michelle held her breath and listened to the turning of pages. Make it soon. Please.

"There's an opening a week from Monday, June nineteenth, at 11:30. Can you make it then?"

"Nothing sooner?" Two weeks might as well be two months. An eternity.

"I'm afraid not. Doctor's really busy these days. Lots of babies born in the summer, you know."

No, she didn't know. She could have filled the Grand Canyon with what she didn't know about having babies. The sudden thought sent panic through her like an Indy race car driver out to set a new record. She clutched the receiver and stared at the ceiling. "Okay. Put me down for the nineteenth."

Kelly said something else before the line went dead, something about a new computer, but beyond that Michelle didn't know. She listened to the dial tone a few moments before hanging up the phone.

"How in the hell am I supposed to get anything done between now and the nineteenth?" She emptied her coffee cup, rinsed it and put it in the dishwasher. As she wiped up the spill from the counter she remembered the clinic. Though she'd decided a long time ago she wouldn't go back, preferring to pretend her baby had begun like most others, they at least deserved a phone call. They said they kept track of the number of siblings resulting from a single donor. She wondered how many they allowed, but she never asked.

She shook her head. No. The phone call would wait for another day. Maybe today would be a good day to clean out her closet. Bag some stuff for Goodwill. Do some laundry. But then what? What would she do tomorrow? And the next day? And the day after that?

She returned to the bedroom and flopped on the bed, indulging the melancholy mood that had settled over her. If only her mother were still alive and she could call her. She'd be excited at the prospect of being a grandmother. A lone tear escaped the corner of her right eye. She rolled on her side, blotting it away with the pillowcase. Her mom and dad had both been only children, too, so there weren't even kindly aunts to share her good news. She closed her eyes and let her mind wander through a collage of familiar faces, until one, then two, came into focus.

Millie and Hazel.

She opened her eyes and smiled into the pillow. She could just imagine them dancing with delight, clapping their hands and squealing over her shoulder as they pulled her to them for a tight embrace. They'd be ecstatic.

But where were they and where was she? Miles apart. Although Toledo wasn't that far away. The idea of hopping in the car and driving there tempted her. They'd written back and

forth once, the pair extending an open invitation. Still, as sweet
as they had been, she barely knew them and they would think
she was crazy if she told them her news.

She sat up and heaved a sigh. That wasn't true. They'd be
tickled pink she thought of them. But she knew what else they'd
think—they'd think the baby was Kevin's. A fresh flow of tears
streaked down her cheeks. Angry with this maudlin mood,
Michelle dried her face on the sheet, pushed off the bed and
strode to her computer in the corner. She flipped the switch and
waited for it to boot up.

Kevin. He was only supposed to be a face. A make-believe
daddy in case this moment ever came. Instead, he was a whole
person. Body and soul. Haunting her to distraction.

She sat down and stared at the blank screen. There was plenty
to do, if she could simply concentrate. She fingered the mouse
on the pad beside the keyboard and pointed to a file. Double-
clicking, she opened the file and struggled to recall where she'd
left off. Millie's and Hazel's smiling faces faded grudgingly.
Maybe someday she'd give them a call or go see them. But not
today. Not for a long while.

Not until Kevin was merely a handsome face and a distant
memory.

As the doctor left the room and shut the door behind him,
Michelle sat dazed on the end of the examining table, clutching the paper sheet to her chest.

The rabbit had indeed died. Deader than a doornail, he'd
said with a paternal smile. It wasn't news. But then it was. Today it was official.

"Two months down and seven to go," she said aloud. As far
away as January sounded, a long list of preparations began
scrolling through her head. First and foremost, she needed a
new apartment. She slid off the table and dressed slowly,
weighing her options. Perhaps a two-bedroom would open up
in her building. She loved the view and the proximity to down-
town—taking the People Mover to Fox Theater and Greektown, going to Hart Plaza for ethnic festivals and a little jazz.
Still, the idea of a big backyard appealed to her. They could get
a puppy and a swing set. She stared out the window, then

laughed at her own folly. A swing set was years off. A crib and diapers were a little more immediate. Visions of terry-cloth sleepers and receiving blankets pranced through her mind as she opened the door and walked to Kelly's desk.

Everyone had left for lunch except Kelly, who seemed deep in thought, hunched over a manual at her new computer. She turned with a start when Michelle leaned on the counter, pulling her checkbook from her shoulder bag.

"Oh! Sorry, Michelle. I forgot you were still here," she said, marking her spot with an appointment card and pushing the book aside.

"Working through lunch?" Michelle glanced at the invoice on the counter and began writing a check.

"It's either that or stay late, and I have better plans for tonight."

Lucky girl, Michelle thought, and handed over her payment.

Kelly took it in exchange for a receipt, then leaned back in her chair. Her eyes asked the question before her lips, and Michelle saw it coming.

"Do you still do computer consulting?"

Michelle took a card from her purse and passed it to Kelly, hoping the young woman would take the hint and call for an appointment. Michelle's mind was still on bibs and booties. She'd purposefully left the day free, thinking she'd take herself out to lunch and then to a bookstore for all the new how-to baby books. She needed a name book, and she'd heard there were lists for stocking a nursery.

"Do you mind? I'll make sure the doctor pays you," Kelly asked.

Somewhere in her daydreaming Michelle missed the first part of the question, but it wasn't hard to figure out since the manual was in Kelly's hands again. With a weary sigh, Michelle walked behind the counter and sat in the proffered chair alongside Kelly. "Okay, what do we have here?"

"It's a new data base program. I thought I understood it, but every time I go to print out this report I get pound signs in some of the columns. I know the data is there, but it doesn't show."

"Ah, an easy one. This will only take a few minutes," Michelle said, relieved it was a common problem she could remedy quickly.

Kelly stood and motioned Michelle into her chair. "I have to run to the ladies room. The service will pick up calls so don't worry if the phone rings. I'll be right back."

Michelle slid over and went to work on the layout screen, dragging the boxes larger to accommodate the data in the established fields. She switched to page preview and scrolled through the report. All fixed. If only they could all be this simple. She was sitting back with a satisfied smile waiting for Kelly to return, when she heard two male voices approaching from somewhere down the hall. From her vantage point, she couldn't see them, but as the sounds grew closer, her heart began thudding in her chest.

*No. It couldn't be. Her mind was playing tricks on her.*

Kelly returned with a smile. "Finished already?"

The two men slowed their pace when Kelly crossed in front of them.

"Kelly... doesn't your boss let you out for lunch?"

"Is that an official chief-of-staff question or idle chatter?" Kelly batted her large blue eyes and smiled coyly at the white-coated man. It looked as if this were an old and comfortable game between them. "What brings you to the professional wing? No surgeries or emergencies in the main building today?"

The chief stopped and folded his arms, leaning with a weary sigh against the counter. "Just needed to see your smiling face," he bantered back. "Actually, we're here to meet the cardiovascular guys in the new wing next door. You must be glad the hammering has come to an end."

"You got that right!" She laughed, then turned to Michelle, looking embarrassed. "I'm sorry. I'm being rude. This is Michelle Purdue. She's a real whiz at computers, and she's helping me out today."

The man extended his hand and introduced himself. "Paul Westerfield. Nice to meet you."

Michelle rose from her chair, feeling the blood drain from her face. She took his hand in hers and said something, but her gaze remained riveted on the second man, hanging back and slightly to the side.

Kelly motioned for the other man to move closer. "And this is Dr. Kevin Singleton."

Singleton. *Dr.* Singleton.

Michelle felt like a sleepwalker, her arms suddenly leaden, her mind not trusting what her eyes took in. She'd had this dream before—running into him at the least-expected moment. But here he was. In the flesh.

Kevin stood there as stunned as she, studying her face, looking for all the world as if he'd fallen into the Twilight Zone. Finally, he stepped closer and reached for her hand.

"Michelle . . ." He swallowed visibly. "Purdue?"

She stared at the familiar fingers, knowing how they'd feel if she clasped them, but also knowing she had no choice. She accepted his shake, which was more like a long, gentle squeeze. He didn't let go for what seemed like the longest time. She could feel Kelly's curious stare, as well as Dr. Westerfield's. But the feeling that burned and sizzled through her was Kevin's touch. Just when she'd thought it was safe to go back in the water, here he was, sinking his teeth into her heart, thrusting another wave of hope over her.

Somewhere in the background she heard a noise. Kevin's hand left hers, but his gaze lingered. As if a hypnotist had snapped his fingers in front of Kevin's face, he blinked hard, stepped back and read the digital display on the beeper clipped to his belt. He rested a hand on the chief of staff's shoulder. "Have to go. Tell the new guys I'll be back another time."

Westerfield nodded, glancing back at Michelle one last time before moving on. He held up a hand and waved without looking back. "Nice meeting you, Michelle. See you later, Kelly."

Michelle dropped down in the chair, still not believing what had just transpired. The flashing cursor on the screen in front of her pulled her back slowly.

*Concentrate, Purdue. Get this done and get out of here.*

"Are you okay?" Kelly said softly over her shoulder.

Michelle fingered the mouse on the pad next to her, delaying conversation, buying time until she remembered how to use her vocal cords. Drawing on every ounce of reserve, she opened the format section of the file in front of her.

"See these boxes here?" she finally asked, ignoring Kelly's question. Kelly pulled a chair up alongside and looked at the screen. Quickly Michelle explained the problem and how to fix it in the future. When she finished, she braved a glance at Kelly, who, as she'd suspected, had a what-was-that-all-about? look on her face. Michelle pretended not to notice and stood. Without further dialogue, she picked up her business card and handed it to Kelly again.

"If you have any questions, give me a call." She flung her bag over her shoulder, forced a weak smile and walked away. Behind her she heard Kelly's delayed response.

"Thanks for your help."

Michelle waved an acknowledgment and kept moving, the need for fresh air rising to emergency proportions. She walked with a no-nonsense stride, for once ignoring the many plants and flowers that lined the way. She unlocked her car, slid behind the wheel and fastened her seat belt. Mechanical moves. No emotion required.

Then she folded her arms against the steering wheel, bent her head and cried. At first a small choke passed her lips, then full-scale sobs, her body shaking out of control. She stopped once, telling herself it was a hormonal thing. She was pregnant. Then she indulged the sobs again.

*Damn you, Kevin. You were supposed to be a fantasy. A faraway, fading memory.*

She pounded the wheel, growling in frustration, angry with her self-indulgence. She had a baby to think about. She shouldn't let herself get so worked up. She turned the key in the ignition and backed out.

"Why?" she asked herself aloud. "Why today?" She'd been so happy with Dr. Wilson's confirmation.

As she drove home, she tried to remember the things she'd planned to do today, but Kevin sabotaged her every thought, with one question overriding all others.

*Now that he knows your name and that you live in the area, will he try to contact you?*

She tightened her grip on the wheel. "Michelle, Michelle. Why are you letting fantasies ruin this special day?"

*And why, oh why, are you praying for this complication in your life?*

# Nine

Kevin checked the number alongside Michelle's name on the board: 712. The security guard approached him suspiciously, opening the locked door between them. Kevin thought of turning around and walking out. It had to be twenty years since he'd played a stunt like this. This wasn't a college prank and he wasn't a kid. He didn't know if he could pull it off without making an ass of himself.

The guard asked, "Can I help, sir?"

"One of my patients called...the flu, I'd guess." Kevin feigned fatigue and held up the black bag in his right hand, then pointed to the name tag affixed to the white coat he never wore out of the hospital. The guard looked semiconvinced.

"Her name's Purdue...in 712." He knew what the guy was thinking so Kevin stole his words. "I debated whether to buzz her, but she sounded pretty sick. No point in making her get out of bed twice. Thought I'd just go up and knock on the door."

The elderly guard rubbed his bearded chin. "Ms. Purdue, huh?" He nodded his head, recollection dawning slowly. "Yep. She didn't look herself at all when she came home this afternoon." He read the name tag again. "We're not supposed to let ya up without buzzing."

Kevin worked at not letting the guy see him sweat.

"Do ya have a card, Dr. Singleton?"

Kevin pulled one from his wallet and handed it over.

"Why don't ya sign my log here and then go on up?"

Kevin scribbled his best prescription signature, then moved to the elevator and punched seven. The door opened. He gave a friendly salute to the guard, stepped in and let a long breath burst through his lips when the door shut. He held his arms out to his sides and studied his costume, a laugh filling the small space. He couldn't remember the last time he'd used this old black bag. And when was the last time a cardiovascular surgeon had made a house call? The elevator stopped and the doors slid open. He stepped out and looked both ways. No one was in the hall. Good. If she slammed the door in his face, there'd be no witnesses to his humiliation.

He walked down the hall, looking at numbers left and right . . . 715 . . . 714 . . . 713 . . . 712 . . . .

He stopped and stared at the number, no longer certain this was a good idea. He knew Michelle wouldn't slam the door in his face, but would she be glad to see him? She hadn't looked glad this afternoon. She'd looked white as a sheet and her hand had trembled when he took it in his. He'd been relieved when his beeper went off, giving him no choice but to leave abruptly. If he hadn't been called away, what would he have said in front of Paul and Kelly? Somehow, a simple "Nice seeing you, again" didn't quite cut it.

He looked at the number on the door and weighed his options. It wasn't too late to turn around and leave. But would the guard mention his name to Michelle tomorrow? What would she think then?

*Okay, Chicken Little, just knock on the door. You've come this far.*

Why couldn't he have called? Or sent a card?

*Because, idiot, you didn't want to do this on the phone, and you didn't want to wait.*

If he waited, he might lose his nerve. He had to know if she wanted to see him again. And he had to see her face when he asked. Besides, he didn't want her to have time to think about a polite response. He wanted the unrehearsed truth.

Shifting the bag to his left hand, he raised his right fist, hesitated one last time, then knocked loudly twice, the sound echoing in the silent hallway.

In the eternity it took for the door to open, he heard the sound of music, and his pulse raced. What if she wasn't alone? What if a man was in clear view? And what arrogance to think she shouldn't be with anyone but . . .

The door opened a crack. Familiar green eyes widened beyond the latched chain. The door shut quickly and he heard the chain sliding. Then the door opened wide.

"Kevin?" she asked, looking as if she'd seen an aberration.

"Michelle?" he asked back, smiling at the memory of their first meeting. She smiled, too, looking more frail than he remembered. Finally, she stepped aside and motioned him in.

"How did you get past Harry?" she asked, standing in the middle of the room in a satiny gray robe, tightening the sash.

Behind her was a wall of glass framing a magnificent view. The setting sun danced and shimmered on the river's surface. He stared beyond her, remembering too much, saying nothing for the longest time. When he looked back to her, she seemed amused as she blatantly studied his attire.

"Oh, this." Kevin held his arms out, looked down and laughed. "This is how I got past Harry. He thinks you're sick."

Michelle laughed, shaking her head. "Do you make a lot of house calls, Doctor?"

"This is a first." He knew she'd heard that line before . . . under different circumstances. "Why is this feeling so awkward?" he asked aloud, giving voice to his thought.

"Because it is," she answered curtly. "When we left the ship we didn't expect to see each other again."

Short and to the point. But she was right. He'd never given her any reason to think he wanted to see her again—a parasitic mistake that had been eating away at him ever since his return. He searched for something clever to say or do that might bridge the growing strain between them.

The bag. God, he'd almost forgotten.

He crossed to her dinette table and deposited the black bag, pulling the contents from it like a rabbit from a hat. "Ta-da!" he sang out as he produced a slightly wilted bunch of purple violets. He held them out, inviting her to come closer.

She did, hesitantly, the smile returning to her face. "I always wondered what you guys kept in those bags." She held the violets to her nose and inhaled.

"I figured if I kept the old thing long enough I'd find a good use for it." This wasn't going at all how he'd envisioned. He'd hoped she'd throw her arms around him, that they'd kiss greedily, hearts racing madly, as they told each other how torturous the time apart had been.

Instead, she turned her back on him in search of a vase. Her flaming hair was longer, braided down her back, a few tendrils loose at her cheeks. Her hips seemed a little more rounded, making his hands feel like magnets, having a mind of their own, wanting to attach themselves to her, allowing his fingers to explore familiar territory.

Michelle pivoted around and leaned on the counter next to the sink. "They're very pretty, Kevin. Thank you." She buried her face in the violets again, avoiding his steady gaze. "We can't just pick up where we left off, you know," she said into the flowers. "Things were different on the ship."

He was starting to feel angry and didn't know why. He'd left her with no last name or whereabouts, no reason to think he wanted to see her again. But damn it, he did, or why else would he be here now? Before her plane ever left Florida, he'd missed her and regretted his decision to remain anonymous. All she had to do was ask Paul what a foul mood he'd been in since his return and she'd know the truth.

The silence stretched unbearably. He had to say something or she'd ask him to leave. There was nothing in her demeanor that encouraged him to think otherwise.

"Michelle . . ."

She raised her eyes but not her head, looking conflicted. He pounced on her uncertainty. "We could start again. . . ."

"Slowly?" She placed the vase in the center of the table and crossed her arms. "No promises? No pressure?"

He watched her eyes grow misty. If she cried he'd be lost. He'd have to put his arms around her and comfort her, tell her everything would be okay. He found himself wishing she'd cry. But she didn't.

"If that's the way you want it." He tried to telegraph another message—that he felt the same about her now as the day they'd parted. Probably more. But he sensed it would spook her and ruin whatever chances he had. He kept his feet rooted in place, wanting desperately to close the space between them. Then she started to laugh and he fell back a step.

"What?" he asked, not seeing the humor in any of this.

She covered her mouth, but continued to laugh behind it. "It's just that . . . well, you look like an old rerun of 'Marcus Welby, M.D.'"

Kevin watched her eyes smile and a surge of hope pumped through him. If he acted quickly, maybe . . .

"Are you doing anything Friday night?" he blurted out, knowing he sounded like a bumbling teenager.

"Are you asking me for a date?"

"Yes."

"No."

"No, you don't want to go out with me? Or no, you're free Friday?"

"Oh, I'm available Friday night, *Doctor*." She smiled mischievously, leaning on his title. "But I'm not free. This is going to cost you. Plenty."

He met the challenge head-on. "Seven okay? Dinner? Dancing?"

"Seven it is," she said, walking to the door and opening it wide.

Kevin took his cue, wanting more, but just as happy to have this first encounter over with.

When he stepped off the elevator a few moments later, Harry greeted him like an old friend. "How's Ms. Purdue? She gonna be okay?"

Kevin patted the man's stooped shoulder and kept moving. "Just got a little bug, Harry. Before long she'll be her old self."

"I'm sure glad ta hear that, Doc," Harry called after him.

God willing, it was true.

*  *  *

"Nice," Michelle said, scanning the tastefully decorated dining room. The booths were high-backed half circles, heavily padded, with rounded ends. Decorative mirrors hung from most walls, reflecting large, airy silk floral arrangements. Though the mauves and teals lent a contemporary air, the feel was art deco, reminding her of old movies. The romantic ones where the tough good guy always got his gal.

"I'm glad you like it." Kevin smiled into his chardonnay, his gaze drifting to his watch. "Band starts soon. Paul says they're good. None of that hard-rock stuff."

Michelle played with the condensation on her water glass wondering how much Kevin had told his friend about the cruise. Not that it mattered; she was simply curious. The drive here had been fairly quiet. She hadn't learned much about this real Kevin. And there was a lot she needed to know before she trusted her feelings, especially . . .

"What's churning behind those worried green eyes?" Kevin asked, bringing her head up with a start.

She emitted a nervous laugh, glancing away, then back. "I know so much about you . . . but so little."

He settled back in the booth and let out a sigh. "Okay. I'm ready. Take your best shot."

She thought he looked as nervous as she felt. The cruise had been easy. This dating business put a whole new spin on things. And there was one big reason for her anxiety.

She was pregnant. And the baby wasn't Kevin's.

In her fantasy world, she allowed herself to think maybe he *was* the father. One of those golden balloons could have been defective. God knew they'd used enough of them. But this was no longer a fantasy. Kevin was real, as was the baby growing inside her.

"Well?" he asked when she said nothing. "Ask me anything. I have no deep, dark secrets." He reached for his wineglass.

She braced herself and went for the big one. "Did you and Jessica have any children?"

Kevin set his glass down without drinking, and she felt her stomach do a somersault. "No," he said, his jaw muscles flexing.

Obviously, she'd touched a sore point. Did his curt response mean he wished they had? If that were the case, maybe he'd be happy with her news...when the time was right to tell him, that is. It was too soon, though. She had to know where this was going first. She'd opened her mouth to ask another question when Kevin held up his hand.

"Let me save you twenty questions." He leaned forward, resting both elbows on the table. "Jessica and I decided our careers were too demanding, that there wasn't time for parenthood along with our other responsibilities."

He finished his wine and eyed her, as if weighing the importance of his next sentence. A warning buzzed in her head and squeezed her heart. She wasn't going to like this, she...

"So that's why I had a vasectomy."

She was right. She didn't like it.

She sat very still, waiting for the shock waves to stop bouncing off her rib cage. The fantasy was over. All the wishing in the world couldn't make Kevin the father—not for this child, or not for any other in the future.

The band started with a soft ballad, one she would have thought romantic if she weren't about to cry. All week she'd looked forward to this night, hoping they could magically find that special place they'd shared on the *Norway*, that this awkwardness would disappear along with unrequited love.

*He doesn't want children.*

One little sentence and everything was over. She watched dancers snuggle closer and her heart pressed against her sternum, the pain as real as the fact that she was carrying another man's child.

Why had they met again? Why couldn't she have held on to the past and at least pretended ...

Kevin stood beside her, his hand outstretched. She didn't want to dance with him, to smell his after-shave, to feel his breath on her ear. She wanted to tell him there was no point in continuing, that she...she...

He took her hand in his and she followed him onto the dance floor. When he found a spot, he turned and pulled her to him, gazing down at her with the same tenderness she'd first seen on deck . . . after the bagpipes. . . .

She pressed her cheek to his chest and closed her eyes, remembering, wishing. It could have been so perfect.

*He doesn't want children.*

His arm circled her back drawing her closer. It felt right. But it wasn't, she reminded herself. She couldn't pretend any longer.

Michelle held him tight, knowing that when this night ended, there would never be another.


Kevin slammed down the phone, drawing stares from the others in the doctors' lounge. He stalked out of the room and down the hall toward the Cardiac Care Unit.

He knew she wanted to take things slowly, but this was ridiculous. After nearly a week's worth of messages left on her machine, she hadn't called back once. If this had been any other woman he would have said "To hell with you" and gone on.

But this wasn't any woman. It was Michelle. The woman he thought he knew better than any other. The woman he thought he . . .

He couldn't bring himself to think the word, let alone say it. He punched in the code and the automated doors to CCU swung open. He sat behind the counter and hunched over a stack of charts, discouraging idle chatter from the staff bustling about the cramped area.

What had gone wrong? She cared about him. He knew she did, the way she'd nestled in his arms on the dance floor—as if she never wanted the night to end. She'd held his hand over the console on the drive back to her place. He'd walked her to the entrance of her building and kissed her, not pressing for too much too soon. She'd kissed him back. Long and hard. And then walked inside. For a moment, he'd thought she'd ask him up. She hadn't seemed to want to let go.

He went over every word he could remember of the entire night again and again. There was only one part that could have bothered her—his vasectomy. Still, if that was important to her, why couldn't she say so? Certainly she'd heard the procedure was often reversed. If having children was a big deal, when they were ready for a commitment, he'd do something about it. She didn't even have to ask.

He read the charts quickly, then stood. All his patients were stable; rounds could wait. But this puzzle scrambling his brain had to be solved. And solved now.

Harry opened the door, his bushy brows bunching with concern. "Doc?"

Kevin brushed by him with a no-nonsense nod.

"Ms. Purdue sick again?" The stooped man shuffled right behind Kevin, following him to the elevator.

"Yes. I have to get right up to her."

"Want me to go with ya?"

Kevin punched the up button and looked back at the old man's worried face. With a hand on Harry's shoulder, Kevin said, "If I need help, Harry, I'll call down. Okay?" He turned and stepped into the elevator.

"Okay, Doc," Harry said as the door closed between them.

The doors opened and Kevin sprang out, sprinting to 712. He pounded on the door loudly, not caring if he roused the whole building.

The door swung open and Michelle met his angry glare. There were dark puffs under her eyes. She looked more than tired, she looked depressed, forlorn. The head of steam he'd built up on the way over seeped out of him. He stepped toward her just as a younger version of Robert Redford strolled around the corner, coffee mug in hand. Kevin pulled back, sizing up the situation.

"Oh!" Pretty Boy said, surprise registering on his young face. He took in the white coat and black bag standing in the doorway, then eyed Michelle. "Are you sick, dear?"

*Dear?* Kevin glared at the little twerp, wishing he was a violent man.

Michelle's gaze darted nervously between the two men. "No, I'm not sick. Are you, Jimmy?"

"No." Jimmy looked confused.

But Kevin wasn't. Not in the least. Suddenly everything seemed perfectly clear. He backed out of the apartment, biting back the crude words on the tip of his tongue. "Sorry," he said between clenched teeth. "Must have the wrong apartment."

Michelle started toward him, but he closed the door between them.

Jimmy rinsed his mug at the sink before picking up his briefcase. He bussed Michelle's cheek, then stopped and held her by the shoulders, gazing down at her fondly. "Thank you, dear."

"You're welcome, Jimmy. I'm glad I could help in some small way."

"As soon as the hospice gets the funding approved, I'll buy the system you suggested and we'll get together then."

"I look forward to it."

"You sure I can't pay you for today?"

"Positive."

A quick hug and Jimmy sashayed out, leaving Michelle alone by the window.

She stared at the Canadian shoreline, her gaze settling on the new casino. If only she were a gambler...

She turned away, refusing to shed another tear. It wasn't like her to treat Kevin so badly—not returning his calls, pretending not to know him when he came to the door. He deserved an explanation, but she didn't have the guts to tell him why it could never work. Perhaps now that he'd made a false assumption about Jimmy, his anger would help him forget her and move on.

*You spineless wimp!*

The truth was, she didn't trust herself to call or see him ever again. He might say it didn't matter that she was pregnant. He might even try to convince her a family was okay with him.

But was it? If he truly wanted a family, he never would have consented to a vasectomy.

*He didn't want children.*

The words kept reverberating in her brain like a lyric from a too-familiar song. In spite of her resolve, a tear trickled down the side of her nose. Angry with herself, she swiped at it as she cleared the papers from the dinette table, moving them to her computer in the bedroom.

Damn it! She had a long-awaited baby on the way. She wouldn't let anything—or anyone—ruin her dream. This baby would be loved and cherished. Her hand circled her tummy and she smiled. It already was.

And no man, no matter how much she cared for him, would cause her one moment of regret for having made this decision.

# Ten

It was the Friday before Labor Day and the hospital cafeteria had more empty chairs than full ones. Michelle watched Kelly polish off her scrambled eggs, then attack a stack of pancakes as if she hadn't eaten in weeks.

Michelle cut up a melon and spread cream cheese on a raisin bagel, stealing occasional glimpses around the abnormally quiet room.

"I'm sorry you couldn't see Dr. Wilson this morning," Kelly said before shoveling in another forkful of carbohydrates and oozing sugar. "I bet you're disappointed."

Michelle swallowed a piece of melon and nodded. "I can't blame him for having to deliver a baby...but, yes, I am disappointed. Today would have been my first ultrasound." She picked up her bagel and scanned the area again when Kelly wasn't looking. Why had she let herself be talked into eating here—of all places?

"I was able to reach all the other patients but you. I'm sorry you made the trip for nothing, but I'm glad you agreed to have something to eat with me. I didn't have time for breakfast this morning and I hate eating alone.'' Kelly finished the last of her pancakes, drank some milk, then smiled at Michelle. "Good thing you don't eat like I do or you wouldn't be wearing those regular clothes.'' She laughed and wiped her mouth with a paper napkin. "No one would ever guess you're four and a half months along.''

"Maybe you can't see it, but I feel it.'' Michelle bloused out her tunic top. "This thing and my loose-fitting jacket hide a lot. I never thought I'd buy pants with an elastic waistband, but lately it's all that fits. Guess I'll have to break down and find real maternity clothes soon.'' Not to mention explain a few things to her customers. Some were pretty conservative and might look askance at an unmarried pregnant consultant, though she thought most would be okay with the news. Those who weren't would help her decide which clients to cut, now that she'd decided to reduce her load.

"Since this is the long Labor Day weekend, you don't have to work, do you?'' Kelly asked.

"No. I'm pretty much caught up.''

"Then this would be the perfect weekend to buy that new wardrobe,'' Kelly said with a wink. "I can't wait till I'm married and have babies. I'll probably start wearing maternity clothes the day after I test positive.'' She laughed, then stopped short when she spotted someone across the room and waved. "You remember Dr. Westerfield?'' she asked, flagging him over without waiting for an answer.

Michelle pressed her back against the chair and kept her eyes straight ahead. Maybe he was alone this time, maybe . . .

Maybe Kevin was right alongside, glowering down at her with gunmetal-gray eyes and a tight jaw.

Westerfield extended his hand. "Michelle, isn't it?''

She caught his cagey glance at Kevin. This guy knew exactly who she was. She wondered how much else he knew.

Michelle took his hand. "Yes . . . So nice of you to remember,'' she said acidly.

Kelly's gaze darted between the three of them, a smile dimpling her cheeks.

Michelle sipped coffee, debating whether she should make her excuses and leave, or wait for them to move on. She knew she shouldn't have come in here. Was this what she'd subconsciously hoped would happen?

Kelly pressed her palms on the table and stood. "Well, I hate to leave this party, but I have to get back." She glanced at her watch as she pushed in her chair. "The sooner I get my paperwork done, the sooner I can start the long weekend." She gave a last lingering look at Michelle, smiled, then turned and walked away.

Paul pulled out a chair. "Mind if we join you?"

Why had he bothered to ask? He was already seated. She should have listened to her instincts and left when she could. "No, not at all," she said, sounding as inhospitable as she felt. She fixed her gaze on the melon rind in the middle of her plate as if it held an answer to her dilemma.

"Come on, Kevin," Paul prodded. "Set your tray down and pull up a chair. Michelle doesn't mind."

Michelle heard the chair slide and saw the tray out of the corner of her eye, but she couldn't have looked up if her life depended on it. Surely Paul knew what he was doing. In fact, it occurred to her that Kelly and Paul had staged this little scene. Kelly, the incurable romantic, probably knew Kevin was a bachelor. And Paul had probably heard every little detail about his friend's Caribbean adventure. How long was he going to pretend otherwise? She heard a beeper go off and felt the breath she'd been holding rush out. Thank God for small favors.

But it was Paul who reached for his belt.

Michelle set her coffee down and slanted him a suspicious glare. If this was a conspiracy, she'd bet anything it was Kelly who'd beeped him. He wouldn't dare leave her alone with—

"Sorry, folks. Have to run."

Paul left the table without so much as a backward glance. Good thing, she thought. If looks could kill, he'd be lying on the floor in a big white heap.

Michelle rotated the cup in her hands and stared at it, refusing to look at Kevin, to be the first to speak. She'd sit here all day like this if she had to. Sooner or later he'd leave and that would be that.

It only took a couple heartbeats for her to realize how foolish and childish she was acting. He'd done nothing wrong.

"Would you like me to move?" he asked, his tone brusque.

She didn't know. Did she? It would definitely be easier than trying to make small talk. His chair scraped backward, and she looked up. "No, wait."

He met her gaze and held it. A fist constricted around her heart and squeezed hard. Behind the angry exterior she saw his pain, pain she had caused, pain much like her own, that he hadn't yet learned to live with.

*Damn.* What could she say that could make things better? Somehow "Let's be friends" didn't seem adequate. She looked back at her plate and the mystic melon. No help there. Eyes averted, she said, "Can we talk awhile? Without getting angry?"

"Depends," Kevin said, not making things any easier.

"On what?"

"On what we talk about."

"Okay." She braved a look in his direction, her pulse racing as it always did when she was with him. "You pick the topic."

He leaned closer and whispered one word. "Jimmy."

"Jimmy?"

"Yeah, Jimmy. You can tell me it's none of my business, but I believed you when you said there was no one else in your life." She could see him straining to keep his voice low. "Was Jimmy before or after the cruise?"

"Before," she said, the corners of her mouth twitching. Now that she knew what he thought she wanted to laugh. His accusation might have made her angry if it weren't so preposterous.

"You think lying is funny?" His voice rose a notch, and now she did get angry.

"I didn't lie to you," she said louder than she'd intended, drawing the attention of a group of nurses at the next table. Propping her cheek on a clenched fist, she let her loose hair fall to one side, hiding her mouth from their view. "Jimmy is a client and a friend." Kevin arched an eyebrow. She wanted to smack the smug look from his face, but she slapped him with a quick response instead. "Jimmy is gay, you idiot."

That left him speechless. Kevin slouched in his chair, crossed his arms over his chest and stared straight ahead. After a moment, he asked, "Have you heard from Millie and Hazel?"

Michelle let out a low laugh and nodded her head. "We wrote back and forth once. Actually, they wrote twice, but I haven't answered the second one yet."

"So *they* knew your last name and address on the ship." It was a statement not a question, and there was a hint of reproach in his voice.

"We agreed . . ."

Kevin held up both hands in surrender. "You're right." There was a long pause before he continued. "Did you ever question that decision?"

Only every day. But what good did it do? Two important facts remained—he didn't want children and she was pregnant by who knew what man.

"Look, Kevin . . . the cruise was magic, something I'll never forget, but . . ."

"But get lost. Is that what you're trying to say?" He looked like a wounded bird with a broken wing.

Instinctively she reached for his hand, covering it with hers—a mistake she realized a second too late. The connection jolted through her as strong as ever. He placed his free hand over hers and she knew she was trapped. She'd never be free of this man, and watching his soulful dark eyes, she couldn't remember why she hadn't given it another chance.

"Kevin," she started, her voice sounding husky to her own ears. "We should talk . . . but not here."

He tightened his hold on her. "When and where?"

She smiled. "You're too easy, you know that?"

"Don't change the subject." His beeper went off and he swore under his breath.

Michelle started to push her chair back. "I know you're busy. I'll just—"

He reclaimed her hand before she could move. "If you don't have to work this afternoon, why don't you hang around? I have to see a patient in Recovery, but it shouldn't take long."

"Then what?" she asked, sensing he had something specific in mind.

"How's your stomach?"

Her free hand covered her swollen midsection under the table. "What do you mean?" Could he know? Had he been poking around hospital records?

"I mean . . . do you get sick at the sight of blood?"

She exhaled loudly. "Oh. That. I don't think so. I watch The Learning Channel on cable all the time. Fascinating stuff. I've seen some pretty gruesome surgeries and never lost my cookies, if that's what you mean."

He squeezed her hand, then stood. "That's exactly what I mean." He checked his watch. "Let's see. Why don't you make it anytime after one o'clock?"

"You don't mean—"

"Why not? I've seen you work behind the computer with Kelly. Aren't you a little curious what I do for a living?"

"Yes, but—"

"Later we'll go someplace quiet, just the two of us, and have that talk. Okay?"

It did sound exciting. Kind of spur-of-the-moment, but then everything had been like that with Kevin. It was one of the many things she . . . she . . .

"Okay," she said quickly, before she could change her mind.

He smiled one of those smiles she'd remembered in the middle of so many wakeful nights.

"Second floor, turn left, end of the hall. I'll leave a pass for you." His beeper went off again as he turned away and stepped up his pace.

*Great. You've really done it now, Purdue.*

The raisins from her bagel felt like basketballs lodged at the back of her throat, each waiting their turn to make it through the narrow tunnel and into the porcelain bowl inches from her sweat-drenched face. God! If only someone would come in and hit her on the back a few times, maybe they'd dislodge. Better yet, club her over the head and put her out of her misery.

Michelle knelt there, waiting for the purge to end, trying to forget the sounds of the saw slicing through bone, the fountain of red that spurt out, Kevin's hands reaching in and pulling out . . .

That did it. She hung on to the sides of the bowl and let nature do its dirty work.

Finally, she sat back on her heels, eyes closed and moaned. The guy on the operating table had to feel better than this, she thought, pulling herself up to the sink. At least he was out cold, something that sounded enviable at the moment.

She cupped cold water in her hands and sloshed some around in her mouth, then splashed her face until she felt as if she might survive. With coarse paper towels, she blotted away the moisture before catching a glimpse of herself in the mirror. Her mascara had run down her white cheeks, giving her a clownish appearance. But there was nothing funny about the way she felt.

A little soap from the canister and more paper towels fixed some of the problem. The blush from her purse and a touch of lipstick made her look almost human again. Her hair was something else. It hung damp and limp about her face. Arms still shaking, she found her brush and an elastic band. Using the last of her energy, she dragged the brush through her hair, pulled it into a ponytail at the nape of her neck and secured it with the band. She didn't even bother to check the results. It didn't matter. She had to sit down before she passed out.

Michelle inched her way down the hall, one hand touching the wall for balance as she looked left and right without moving her head. A chair, an empty bed—even a coffin would do. Even though she didn't expect to find one of those, she wasn't particular at the moment. The floor was starting to look good.

"Can I help you?" An angel in white appeared at her side and Michelle made an effort to smile.

"Need to lie down."

The angel put an arm around Michelle's waist and ushered her somewhere.

"Are you alone?"

"Dr. Singleton—"

"He's in surgery right now—"

Michelle held up a hand to stop the flow of words. The mere mention of surgery conjured up images best forgotten.

"There's a lounge with a sofa right around the corner."

Michelle trudged along, eager for the sight of something long and horizontal. When she spotted it, she moved directly to it and gingerly lowered herself onto her side, bringing her knees up to her stomach. She closed her eyes and exhaled slowly, feeling as if she might live after all. A short time later, she felt a blanket cover her and a cool, fresh pillow slip under her cheek. She opened her eyes and whispered, "Thank you," then quickly closed them again.

"Do you need to see a doctor?"

Michelle shook her head.

"Should I tell Dr. Singleton where to find you when he's—"

Michelle opened her eyes and said, "Yes, please," cutting her off. "You're very kind. Can I stay here for a while?"

"As long as you'd like. I'll check back later and see how you're doing."

Michelle floated somewhere between the here and now and deep sleep, not sure how much time passed, not caring. Each time she started to come around, she thought she'd rest a little longer, only to fall back under. Her dreams were all in color, mostly red on white, sometimes with stick people in aqua with masks over their faces.

She felt the sofa dip in the middle, and then a hand trailed up and down her arm. The hand felt soothing and warm. Someone said, "Ummm . . ." and she awoke slowly at the sound of her own voice.

"Are you feeling better?"

She nodded, eyes still closed.

"I could get you some Compazine if you still feel nauseous."

Michelle sat up with a start, her brain bouncing off the sides of her skull. When her vision cleared, she saw that it was Kevin, not the angel, who sat beside her.

He put his arms around her and pulled her close. "I'm so sorry, Michelle. I guess that wasn't one of my brighter ideas." He stroked her back soothingly.

She could smell soap; his hair was still damp. She glanced down his top. It was a fresh, clean one. He must have showered and changed.

"How's your patient?"

"He looks better than you do," Kevin said.

"What time is it?" she asked into his chest, relishing the feel of him next to her.

"Almost six."

She pulled back and looked him in the eye. "No! I couldn't have slept that long."

He tucked a stray hair behind her ear and looked worried. "Is there something else wrong ... besides what just happened?" Michelle averted her gaze. "Have you been sick lately? The flu or something?"

She brushed nonexistent lint off his sleeve. "Oh, I've been feeling a little punk. Nothing to worry about."

"As long as you're here, I think you should see someone."

"No!" she practically shouted, then tried calming herself. Another wave of nausea left her swaying as she clutched at her rumbling stomach. She couldn't be sick again. There wasn't anything left.

"I insist. You look like death warmed over."

"Thanks," she said sarcastically, though that was exactly how she felt.

"Come on." He pulled her up by the elbow.

She leaned against him and groaned aloud. Another raisin must have been holding out for just this unpropitious moment.

He started to drag her off. "We're going to Emergency and have you checked out."

Michelle pulled her arm free. "No. I don't need a doctor. I just want to go home and go to bed." Her stomach lurched and she looked past him to the rest room door. She didn't have time to argue, unless he wanted to see her brunch again.

Kevin grabbed her forearm and tugged her in the opposite direction. "Damn it, Michelle. We can argue later. Something's wrong—"

She broke free again, moving quickly toward the rest room. Kevin caught up and blocked her path.

"Kevin, please." She clamped her hand over her mouth and gagged, then swallowed hard, tasting the bile. "I know what's wrong and you can't help. Just let me by." She pushed at his shoulder, but he didn't budge.

His anger cooled instantly. His dark, determined eyes by turns looked worried and suspicious. "What do you mean? What's wrong with you?"

This wasn't the time, or the place. But she had to get past him. Now! "I'm pregnant and I'm going to throw up all over you if you don't move this instant." He stepped slowly aside and she rushed past him.

Ten minutes of dry heaves and she pulled herself back to the sink. She had to find Kevin and explain. What must he be thinking? She rinsed her mouth and skipped the cosmetic repairs. How would she begin? Would he believe her? She crumpled the paper towel, tossed it into the trash and opened the door. An orderly pushed a gurney toward her. She stepped aside. When he passed, she looked left and right. Kevin was nowhere in sight. She raced back to the lounge, knowing before she rounded the corner that he wouldn't be there.

She sat heavily in the nearest chair, absently fingering the heart-shaped pendant that hung from her neck. She stared at the spot on the sofa where he'd held her and comforted her only minutes earlier. Who could blame him for leaving?

The nurse who had ministered to her earlier poked her head in the doorway. "You feeling better?"

Not really. "Yes. Thank you . . . for everything."

"Is there anything else you need?"

Kevin. She needed Kevin. "Could you page Dr. Singleton for me?"

"Sure. When he calls the desk, what would you like me to tell him?"

That I'm sorry. Please come back so I can explain. "Ask him—" She almost said "to meet me back here," but then she reconsidered. Her apartment would work much better. It was quiet, more private. "Ask him to call Michelle at home in about a half hour."

"You sure you can get yourself home alone?"

"Positive." She stood slowly, hoping she looked better than she felt. "Thank you again for your help."

The nurse gave a little dismissive wave, then said, "I'll go beep the doctor. You go home and take care of yourself." She smiled and left Michelle wobbling in the center of the room.

# Eleven

"Hi, Harry." Michelle kept moving, eager to shed her clothes, brush her teeth and talk with Kevin, not necessarily in that order.

Harry tipped his cap as she raced by. "Ya still lookin' a little under the weather, Ms. Purdue, if ya don't mind me sayin'."

"I don't feel very well, Harry." She punched the up button a second time for good measure. "In fact, Dr. Singleton might be stopping by this weekend." The elevator slid open and she added, "You can let him up anytime without buzzing me. Okay, Harry?"

"Okay, Ms. Purdue. Take care now."

Michelle smiled when she was out of view. At least Kevin didn't have to wear that silly uniform to get by Harry anymore. The doors slid open on seven and Michelle stepped out, the short-lived smile fading.

Would Kevin even *try* to get past Harry?

She shook her head and pushed one leg in front of the other until she reached her apartment and let herself in. Before she did anything else, she checked the answering machine next to her computer. The red light held steady. No calls.

Good. This was good, she decided. She hadn't missed his call. A shower sounded wonderful, but she wouldn't hear the phone over the water. She walked to the bathroom, wet her toothbrush, spread the paste and brushed her teeth with the water off, turning it on briefly to rinse. Next, her clothes went into the hamper, and then she ran a little hot water at a slow trickle and refreshed herself at the sink with a washcloth. A long Pistons T-shirt hung behind the door. She grabbed it and pulled it over her head, inside out, not wanting to think about basketballs any more today.

Then she sat in her favorite recliner in front of her favorite view and waited.

And waited.

And waited.

The setting sun reflected off the Detroit River and the lights of Ontario dotted the shoreline on the far side.

Eventually, the water turned as black as the sky, with only an occasional sliver of moonshine peeking through passing clouds. Michelle's apartment was dark, too, but not as dark as her mood. She'd thought she'd convinced herself to go this journey alone.

Until this afternoon.

When Kevin had held her hand between his so possessively. When he'd cradled her in his arms and made her feel whole again. Ever since the cruise, she'd felt half. No matter how many times she lied to herself, half had been missing.

Until this afternoon.

Now he was gone, again. She'd left two more messages for him in the intervening hours and still no call.

*Face it, Purdue. You really blew it this time.*

Saturday dragged on mercilessly. Michelle paced, feeling like a caged animal in too small a space. Angry, more with herself than with Kevin, she called his service again.

"I'm sorry," came the disembodied voice. "He's out of town until Tuesday. If this is an emergency, another doctor is covering."

Yes, it was an emergency. But only one heart specialist could fix it. "No. That's okay. It can wait till Tuesday."

Like hell it could. She wasn't going to sit around here another minute hoping the phone would ring. She hung up the phone, then rifled through her closet for something comfortable to wear, settling for a lightweight sweat suit. It was about time she went shopping. Maybe a hot fudge sundae would help, too. On her way home she'd stop at the video store and stock up for the long weekend. On Sunday, she'd take the People Mover to Greektown and go to mass at St. Mary's. And pray for an answer to this mess she'd made for herself.

But for now, shopping and chocolate would have to make do.

On Wednesday, when Kevin still hadn't called, Michelle drove to the hospital before lunch. She'd eat in the cafeteria and watch for him. If she didn't spot him there, she'd go to the surgical waiting room and hope there was a patient's family waiting to see him. One way or the other, she'd find him before the day ended. He deserved an explanation. Beyond that, if his ego couldn't deal with the situation, then so be it. Her own pride wouldn't let him think there had been another man. He had to know the truth, though she realized accepting it would be a whole new ball game.

Michelle refilled her coffee and returned to the table, glancing at the clock on the wall: 1:15. He could've eaten in the doctors' lounge, she supposed. Just because he'd eaten here last week with Paul didn't mean he did every day. She scanned the tables one last time, finished her coffee, then asked directions to the surgical waiting room.

When she found it, the volunteer at the reception desk asked, "Which patient are you waiting for?"

"None, actually," Michelle said, feeling embarrassed for some reason. Why did she care what this stranger thought? She had a mission. "Can you tell me if Dr. Singleton has a patient in surgery?"

The white-haired woman studied Michelle for a moment before consulting her list, as if trying to decipher what ulterior motive might be hiding behind the question. Grudgingly she flipped through pages, being careful to hold the clipboard at an angle so that Michelle couldn't read it. She stopped suddenly and asked, "Why do you want to know?"

So I can explain I didn't have sex with another man besides him. What business was it of hers? "I need to discuss a patient with him," she said, masking her impatience. "I thought I might catch him here when he stops by."

The woman thrust out her chin and pursed her lips, clearly impressed with the importance of her nonpaying job. "I'm sorry. I can't give you that information."

Michelle struggled to hold her temper. "Perhaps you can give me directions to the chief of staff's office, then."

The woman looked worried all of a sudden, as if she were about to be reported to the principal's office. "Um...let's see." She found a brochure and turned a map in Michelle's direction, spelling out the directions hurriedly.

"Thank you." Michelle accepted the brochure, smiled a perfunctory smile and departed.

Kevin and Paul were friends—that much had been obvious when they met again last week. Still, what was she going to say to this man when she found him? Had Kevin told him about the cruise? And that now she was pregnant?

Michelle found Paul's office and was greeted by a friendlier woman.

"Can I help you?"

Before Michelle could answer, she heard the laughter of two men coming from behind a closed door. Then the door opened and Kevin strode out, Paul right behind him. Seeing Michelle, Kevin stopped and Paul nearly ran into his back. The smiles disappeared from both men's faces.

Paul recovered first. "You two can use my office if you'd like. I'll be in a meeting for the next hour or so." He raised his eyebrows at Kevin with an almost indiscernible nod toward his office, then excused himself.

Kevin's jaw muscles were working overtime. For a moment, Michelle thought he might walk out without acknowledging her presence. Instead, he said, "I only have a few minutes," then turned back in the direction he'd just come from. Michelle followed, closing the door behind her.

Kevin crossed his arms and leaned against the front of Paul's desk, his dark gaze almost indifferent, not only to whatever she might say, but to her very existence.

"I know how it must look to you...." She couldn't look him in the eye. She turned and sat in one of the side chairs, holding her arm out to indicate the other one next to her. "Please?"

"I'm comfortable right here," he said, not moving an inch.

He wasn't making this easy. She'd thought all weekend about how to tell him, but he looked like he might have thirty seconds of patience left before he bolted. She opted for the direct approach, forgetting her rehearsed words. "I was artificially inseminated the morning the cruise left." Kevin rolled his eyes, then stared at his shoes. "Really!" She pressed on. "I've wanted a baby for years. I planned this for a long time before we met and—"

He pushed off the desk and glared down at her. "Right. The immaculate conception." He looked at his watch, then back to Michelle, his eyes filled with rage.

Michelle pushed out of the chair, bringing herself within touching distance. She could feel her own anger building up a good head of steam, which made her eyes cloud over. *Damn.* She blinked back the tears that always came when she was this furious, this frustrated. She didn't want him feeling sorry for some weeping woman. She just wanted him to believe her.

With another step to the side, she stood directly in front of him and looked him in the eye, hoping he would see the truth in her face. More than anything, she longed to reach out and touch his cheek, but she was afraid to move, afraid he might flinch, pull away. He stared her down as if she were some loathsome malpractice attorney here for a little chat.

"If that's it, I have work to do." He stepped sideways, purposefully avoiding body contact, and left the room.

Michelle stared at the space he'd occupied, numb with a sadness she hadn't felt since her parents' deaths. There was nothing more she could do. She'd told him the truth, but he didn't believe her. Until this very moment, she'd hung on to a thread of hope that they might have a chance together. The thread had just broken and nothing was left but a large, painful knot.

Slowly she turned and left the room.

Michelle didn't remember the drive home. Once inside her apartment, she roamed from room to room, feeling lost. Everything had been so well planned—charting her fertile cycle for over a year, finding a clinic that needed computer help, observing the place and the process of insemination, then actually becoming a patient. Even the cruise had been calculated to help her relax and make it work.

It had worked, all right. Everything had worked.

Except controlling her feelings for Kevin.

The video on her VCR rolled the credits and she couldn't remember a thing about the story. She sat down and hit the power button on the remote control, then stared at the blank gray screen. She'd allow herself this one last night of self-pity. Tomorrow it was work as usual. Not life as usual. That would take some time.

A light rap on the door brought Michelle to her feet. In all the time she'd lived here, only one person had gotten as far as her door without buzzing first. Heart pounding, she sucked in air through her mouth and raced to the entry. She caught a glimpse of herself in the oval mirror that hung on the wall. Damn! Her hair was a sight. And no makeup. The knee-length T-shirt was faded and wrinkled. Her rounded midriff kept it from hanging straight, the front riding higher than the back.

Michelle squared her shoulders and heaved a long sigh. "Oh, well," she muttered to her reflection, then opened the door.

A white-coated Kevin filled the doorway, a black bag in one hand and a large pot of yellow chrysanthemums in the other. The stunned expression on his face made him look like he'd just pulled the pin on a grenade. She could imagine what he was thinking—did he run for cover or wait for her to slam the door in his face? Or there was another possibility—why was he pursuing this barefoot and pregnant woman?

Michelle looked at him again and thought she saw embarrassment, uncertainty. Hesitantly he held out the potted plant as if it were a peace offering and she took it.

A nervous laugh stuck in her throat and she started to cough.

Kevin dropped his bag and began slapping her on the back not too gently. When the cough turned to a laugh he stepped back.

Michelle caught her breath and asked, "When are you going to stop wearing that ridiculous costume?" He slumped visibly, the tension seeming to escape his body on a long sigh. "I told Harry you might stop by . . . to let you up anytime without buzzing."

He cocked an eyebrow and slanted her a puzzled look. "You were that certain I'd come?"

The smile vanished from her lips as she stared at her bare feet. "No."

He bent over so that his face was level with hers. "Do you think we could continue this conversation inside?"

Michelle jumped back and opened the door the rest of the way. Kevin picked up his bag and strode in, acting a little more confidently.

"I should go put something else on," she said, as much to herself as to Kevin.

He sat on the sofa and called over his shoulder. "Don't on my account."

She put the flowers on the dinette table, walked around the opposite end of the sofa and sat sideways facing him, pulling her feet up under her, tucking her T-shirt under her knees.

When she couldn't stand the silence another second, she blurted out, "Let me explain. . . ."

"No!" He raised his voice and she pulled back, clamping her mouth shut. If he was angry and he didn't want her to talk, then why was he here? The hope she'd allowed herself to feel was slowly turning to anger.

Kevin turned sideways at the far end and faced her, looking more agonized than angry. Something warred behind his eyes as he struggled to find the right words.

"I'm the one who needs to explain," he began.

Whatever his news, it didn't look happy. She braced herself for something; she couldn't imagine what.

"It's about Jessica," he said, gazing out at the river.

His voice sounded distant and cold, as though he were speaking to an empty room. Michelle crossed her arms under her breasts and fought a chill.

"When we first married, we were both in graduate school and there wasn't time or money to start a family. But later, after we got our practices going, I just assumed she'd want children.'' He glanced at Michelle, then back to an anonymous spot on the water. ''Shortly before our divorce, she asked me to get a vasectomy. She said she didn't want to interrupt her career, that she didn't think she'd ever be able to make children a priority.

''I was stunned for a while . . . in denial I guess. I put off doing anything about the situation, hoping it was a phase she was going through, that she'd change her mind. Well, she didn't.'' He looked back to Michelle and she held his gaze.

Was she supposed to say something here? If so, what? That she understood now why he was so angry with her? Kevin looked back to the river again, taking his time with whatever else he had to say. And she could see now, by the set of his jaw, that there was more.

''I had the vasectomy she wanted.''

Michelle knew that part, but she was stunned into silence by what he said next.

''Not long after I had it done, she strolled in one day and made her little announcement. I'd lost a patient just hours before and I made it clear I wasn't in the mood for a long discussion. So she came right to the point.''

He turned his head toward Michelle. She didn't like the cold, surly curve of his lips.

''I can still hear Jessica's voice. She sounded so cold—straightforward, clinical, totally void of emotion. She could've have been giving me the weather report.''

Kevin swallowed visibly, as if the memory left a bitter taste in his mouth, one he was still gagging on. ''She said, 'I'm pregnant by one of my partners in the firm. I'd like a divorce as quickly as possible so he and I can marry before our child is born.' '' He poked at the afghan on the cushion between them and kept his eyes riveted on it. ''Funny thing is . . . I didn't know she was unhappy, let alone having an affair.''

Michelle sat quietly, not moving until she was sure he'd finished. When he finally looked her in the eye, she expected to see hurt or anger. What she saw was a plea for understanding and forgiveness. ''So when you told me you were . . .''

Michelle closed the distance between them, taking his damp hands in hers and squeezing them hard. ''It's okay. I understand.'' Her arms ached to hold him, but she held back, sensing it was too soon. Now she knew why he had reacted so strongly. His eyes lingered on hers, a question aching behind them.

"I'm not Jessica, Kevin. What I told you is the truth. There's been no one else." And she doubted there ever would be, though she couldn't say it. But where did all this fit? Even if he said he loved her, which he hadn't, was there any future for them? She felt dizzy, overloaded with information she couldn't process. One second she wanted him to hold her and tell her everything would be okay. The next she wished he'd leave so she could sort things out. Alone.

He pressed her cheek against his chest and stroked her hair.

Darkness fell over the room and neither of them moved or spoke. Almost by tacit agreement, they realized enough had been said for one day.

When Michelle fell asleep snuggled against him, Kevin eased himself off the sofa, propped a throw pillow under her head and covered her with the afghan. He scribbled a short note next to the phone, then let himself out, locking the door behind him.

# Twelve

---

Michelle woke about midnight, letting her mind drift awhile with images of Kevin—on the cruise, on the beach at Magens Bay, in the hospital when she'd learned he was a doctor.

A surgeon. She'd known on the ship that he wasn't in construction. His hands were uncallused, with a certain grace yet boldness, that she hadn't been able to explain. She opened her eyes and waited for them to adjust to the darkness.

A faint glow came from somewhere. She stood and arched her back, noticing the light under the microwave had been turned on. Curious, she stumbled toward it, still half-asleep, but hoping she'd find a note. She wasn't disappointed. On the back of a paper towel, Kevin had scribbled a few words.

Dear Michelle,
I could use a few days to digest all this—I imagine you could, too. I don't know where this is going. Do you? But I know I want to see you again.
If it's okay with you, I'll pick you up Saturday night at 7:00—dress casually. If you'd rather not, let me know.

I'll try to understand.

Kevin

Michelle read the note a second time, more slowly, trying to read between his words, but she found nothing that changed her mind. She'd see him Saturday night. And he was right—she needed time to think, too. Like Kevin, she didn't know what the future held for them. Would he want to marry her? If he ever asked, would she say yes? If there were only the two of them to consider, she already knew the answer.

Her hand circled her swollen belly and she felt a little kick. It was happening more often now and she cherished the slightest movement. She took Kevin's note with her to the recliner facing the window and settled in, raising the footrest to the lowest setting. Smiling, she clutched the paper to her chest with one hand and felt the baby churning with the other.

"What do you think, little one? I'm sure you'd like a daddy." A bigger kick pushed against her hand and she laughed. "Was that a yes or a no?"

But more importantly, she thought, gazing at the lights of Windsor across the river, was Kevin that daddy?

Michelle yawned as she pushed out of the chair and headed for bed. Maybe by Saturday things would seem clearer. She climbed under the covers remembering what else she had planned for Saturday—her rescheduled ultrasound. And before that came the amniocentesis. What a week this would be! Cradling her belly in both arms, she floated effortlessly into a deep and dreamless sleep.

The days passed quickly, filled with clients and all their related glitches, leaving Michelle exhausted each night. Kevin lurked at the back of her thoughts, but she couldn't bring herself to examine the plethora of questions that needed answering.

Tonight she'd see him. Perhaps magically she'd know what to say once they were together in the flesh. So to speak. She didn't know if she was ready for anything physical yet. One touch, one kiss, and reason would be overpowered by the rush of blood to her lower extremities. Lying here now on the examining table, she could feel her nipples harden, pressing against the thin cotton top she'd worn for this special occasion. Erotic memories ebbed and flowed until Dr. Wilson entered the room. Then all thoughts were on the monitor he wheeled through the door.

"Ready for some moving pictures?" he asked, plugging in the equipment.

As eager as she'd been for this day to arrive, she felt nervous, worried that all would be well, which seemed irrational. She'd had the amniocentesis earlier. If there was a problem, he wouldn't be smiling now.

"Michelle? Is something wrong?"

"N-no." She stammered. "I was wondering about the amniocentesis."

"Would you like to discuss the results before the ultrasound?"

"Should we?" There was something in the way he asked the question that made her think he knew something she ought to know.

He patted her arm and smiled down at her reassuringly. "There's nothing wrong, Michelle. Why don't we watch some movies?"

Biting her top lip, she nodded.

"Okay now, just lay back and relax." He raised her top to expose her belly, then uncapped a tube of jelly. "This is going to be cold," he said, squeezing a large, clear glob below her navel. She shivered as he rubbed the goo all over, then picked up a corded instrument that looked something like a man's electric razor, but rolled over her belly like a computer mouse. The doctor turned the screen toward him, obscuring her view, his gaze intent on the image as the mouse moved from one spot to another.

Why didn't he let her see? There was something wrong. She looked from his face to her belly, then back to his face, watching his unreadable expression. Panic, and the gallon of water she'd had to drink before getting on the table, pressed her limits. It was a contest to see which would give way first—her tear ducts or her bladder. The hand on her belly stopped moving.

"There," he said, looking like the cat that swallowed the canary. "Now you can look." He turned the monitor toward her.

Shades of gray and an occasional jiggle. She didn't know what she'd expected, but this wasn't it.

The doctor pressed a button and a section zoomed larger. He pointed to a medium gray mass and said, "Watch this."

She saw a small flutter and tried to determine what she was seeing.

"That's the heart," he said.

She looked harder, convincing herself it looked like a heart.

He pointed to another area. "Now watch this."

She did as she was told and saw another flutter, the same as the first. "How can you tell what you're looking at? It looks just like the heart." She studied it intensely, trying to discern the difference.

"That's because it is a heart," he said, watching her expression turn from confusion to shock to awareness, all in the space of seconds.

"No... You can't mean ... Are you trying to tell me ... ?"

He smiled broadly. "Twins."

Now that pushed her over the edge. "Can I go to the bathroom?"

He laughed and said, "Sure." He held her arm as she sat up and swung her legs over the side.

A moment later and several ounces lighter, Michelle lay back on the table and asked, "Can I see some more?"

"Whenever you're ready."

She hiked up her top and exposed her jelly-smeared tummy so the doctor could continue his excursion with the mouse.

"Did you decide whether you want to know the sexes?"

Michelle looked away from the monitor, afraid he might point to something that would ruin the surprise. She was curious, yes, but for some old-fashioned reason she wanted to wait. "If I look back at the screen will it be obvious?"

The doctor chuckled. "Not unless you mistake an umbilical cord." Michelle braved a glance while he explained. "The babies have to be positioned a certain way to determine their sex, which isn't the case right now. But the amniocentesis results are in that folder," he said, nodding toward the counter behind him.

She couldn't take her eyes off the screen. These little gray amoebae were her babies. Babies! Two. She'd have to order a second crib....

"I take it you don't want to know, then," he said after a while.

"I might change my mind, but I think I'll wait." Michelle watched the screen, thinking she saw two distinct forms now.

"Ah, here's a good one. I'll print this one out for you."

She was so in awe of what she was seeing and the news she'd just heard that the questions she'd prepared earlier no longer seemed important. Except one. Accepting the priceless negative the doctor handed her, she stared at it and asked tentatively, "The tests from the amniocentesis . . ."

"Not to worry. The alpha fetal protein test was normal. Everything is fine." He held out a hand and helped her to a sitting position. "There's just one thing."

He eyed her in a way that made her feel like a recalcitrant child. Her heart climbed behind her tonsils. "What, Doctor?"

"Have you been eating much?" She smoothed her top over her sticky belly and avoided eye contact. "That's what I thought," he continued sternly. "If you're worried about your figure, forget it for a while. These babies need lots of fruits and vegetables and milk. Even starches. You told me you swim and walk a lot, so you'll get your figure back in no time."

She wasn't worried about her waistline. That was not at all why she hadn't been gaining much weight. But she knew her love life, or lack of it, was no excuse, either. Beginning today, she'd feed her little ones, whether she was in the mood or not.

The doctor scribbled a few lines on her record, then closed the folder against his chest and smiled. "Twins could come early, so let's make sure they're well fed, okay?"

"Okay." Michelle nodded, feeling guilty as he left the room. She lifted the ultrasound negative closer to her face and studied the little shapes until her eyes blurred. She was going to be a mother. She'd known it for months, but seeing them—*them*—she still couldn't believe there were two. Seeing them made it real.

Slowly she slid off the table and somehow found the way to her car. An autumn breeze stirred fallen leaves around her legs as she fumbled with the keys.

Halfway home she remembered tonight's date with Kevin and smiled.

"I wonder what he'll say when I tell him I'm expecting twins." She laughed aloud, already picturing his face.


"You're *what?!*" Kevin practically shouted, his eyes widening, his jaw dropping to the floor. He'd thought he had the situation under control, thought he knew what he was dealing with. But *twins?* He turned and paced to the window where he stared blindly at the river. Then, worried he'd probably blown it again, he strode back to Michelle and cupped his hands on her shoulders.

"How do *you* feel about this news?" She looked pale and drawn. Worry replaced shock as he stooped to meet her level gaze. "Talk to me, Michelle. Are you all right?"

Finally, she smiled. "I guess my reaction wasn't much different than yours. I was stunned at first, but I'm starting to get more excited about it as the shock's wearing off. I'm fine, really. The doctor says I have to eat more, though."

Kevin heaved a relieved sigh and pulled her to him. "Is that all?" After he caught his breath, he stepped back and gazed down at her. "At least that part I can help with. You ready to go?"

"Yes. But you haven't told me where—"

"Just grab your purse and keys, or whatever you need, and let's go. You'll find out soon enough." He flashed her a confident smile.

Michelle took a trench coat from the closet, stuffed her keys in a small handbag and hooked her arm in his. She slanted an impish grin in his direction. "I guess this is a day for surprises, huh?"

"All good ones, though," he said in his most reassuring voice, hoping it compensated for his initial reaction. He didn't care if she was expecting quintuplets—somehow they'd make this work. Enough sleepless nights had convinced him his plan was a sound one. One more baby didn't sway his decision.

They drove north on Jefferson Avenue in companionable silence, stealing glimpses at one another from time to time, until they reached Lakeshore Drive in Grosse Pointe. Kevin watched Michelle taking in the scenery, swiveling her head from side to side. On the left were large estates set back from the road, tucked behind mature trees, landscaped to perfection. On the right was a rare stretch of Lake St. Clair, close to the road, unobstructed by homes or country clubs. The last rays of sunset danced and shimmered off the glassy surface of the water as they turned left and wound their way west to Kevin's home.

He'd spent the afternoon tidying up, wandering from room to room, viewing each as Michelle might when she saw his home for the first time. He hadn't realized how drab and cold the place looked until today. He never spent much time there, unless it was to sleep or catch up on some reading in the library. There were no plants or signs of a woman's touch. It was clean, spacious and utilitarian. That was about all he could say about it. As he pulled into the long circular drive, he wondered if he'd made a mistake bringing Michelle here. Maybe an elegant restaurant with a piano playing in the background would have been more romantic, more suitable for the occasion.

He stopped the car and turned to her tentatively. "I've been to your home several times. I thought you might like to see where I live." He felt like a teenager again. He'd slept with this woman, knew every inch of her beautiful body. Yet now he felt nervous and unsure of himself, as if this were their first date. It was in a way—the first since the cruise, anyway.

"Do I get to see the inside? Or is this it?"

Kevin pulled himself back to the present, only to see Michelle's smiling face studying his frozen posture. Without answering her question, he got out of the car and strode around to the other side, sucking in the crisp fall air in the process. He opened her door and held out a hand, which she took, the corners of her mouth curving upward.

Michelle eyed the gracefully curved cobblestone walk leading to an arched front door. Ivy clung to the brick chimney tucked behind the long, sloped roof of the Tudor entrance. The house spread right and left, some parts receding, others protruding, all at angles pleasing to the eye. She knew her mouth had dropped open as she took it all in, but she couldn't move. A few orange-and-red leaves blew across the perfectly manicured lawn, with most still clinging to countless maples and oaks. Evergreens, some taller than the house, were strategically placed, providing privacy from the neighboring homes on either side. She blinked hard, but it was all still there. She had stepped through Alice's looking glass and was in another world.

Kevin took her arm and escorted her up the walk, opening the door to a massive foyer. Dark, highly polished hardwood floors invited her in. Without thinking, she wiped the bottoms of her shoes on a thick Persian rug, then quickly stepped aside and inspected the spot. Kevin laughed softly behind her as he hung up her coat.

She glanced over her shoulder and felt a blush creep up her neck. "What?" she asked a little defensively.

He took her hand and squeezed it. "You look like a little girl who just found Oz."

Michelle looked around her, still stunned by the size and beauty of his home. "I don't know why I'm surprised." She chuckled nervously. "You are a surgeon." She looked up at the high coved ceilings and ornate woodwork. "I guess I didn't think about how—" She almost said "wealthy you must be," but she didn't. "How well you must live."

He laughed. "When you see the rest of the place, I'm afraid you'll discover I don't really *live* here. It's just a place to sleep once in a while."

Michelle pulled her head back and lifted an eyebrow, doubting anyone could own such a home and not enjoy it. "Uh-huh."

"Really. Want the grand tour?"

She nodded her head, then started without him, stepping down into the living room, crossing immediately to the fireplace. The slab under the grate was clean. It looked as though it had never been used. She spun around and surveyed the furnishings—provincial and brocade. Beautiful but not inviting. Certainly not Kevin. She let him take her hand and lead her through a maze of rooms on the first floor, until they looped

their way back to a formal dining room. There she saw the long
mahogany table. Two place settings, replete with crystal, ster-
ling silver and bone china, waited at the far end.

"We're eating here?" she asked, surprised once again.

"Yes. If you don't mind."

"That depends." She slanted him a curious look.

"On?"

"Who's cooking."

"Well, I am, of course. You're my guest." He feigned an
offended look, but she thought he was probably feeling a little
smug, being a busy surgeon and still knowing how to cook.

"May I ask what we're having?" She sniffed the air for a clue
but found none. Maybe it was being delivered later.

"Promise you won't laugh?" Suddenly he looked embarrassed.

She crossed her heart and smiled at his handsome face.

"Pot roast," he said sheepishly.

"I love pot roast," she said, snuggling closer to his side. "I
rarely make it, since it's too much for one person and I'm not
very good about using up leftovers. What all did you put in it?"
She felt Kevin relax a notch. He still seemed tense, though, unlike her poised, assured self, she laughed inwardly.

"Potatoes, carrots, seasonings and lots of onions—all in one
big pot. Is that how you make it?"

She sniffed the air again. "Exactly. But you know it takes a
while. When did you plan to start it?"

He puffed out his chest and smiled. "Just this afternoon I
read the manual on time-bake." He looked at his watch, then
back to her puzzled face. "Another forty-five minutes and it
should be— What's wrong?"

"I love the smell of pot roast cooking. Don't you?"

Kevin breathed in deeply. "Yes, I— How come I don't smell
anything?"

Michelle shrugged, almost certain of the answer. His smug
expression disappeared along with the rest of him as he raced
for the louvered swinging doors at the back of the dining room.
Before she could count to three, she heard a string of oaths
coming from the kitchen. She decided to brave his foul mood

and join him. The oven door was open, but clearly no heat emanated from it.

"I set the start time, the stop time and the temperature."

"So what's the problem?"

"I forgot to turn the knob to bake."

Michelle started snickering.

Kevin tried valiantly to stay angry, but the corners of his mouth quivered. "I'm glad you think it's funny. Now it'll be hours before we can eat."

"We'll figure out something to pass the time." The words were no sooner out of her mouth than she realized how provocative they sounded. "I mean...well...do you have a VCR?"

"You want to watch a video?" he asked, cocking his head to one side.

"Sure. Why not? By the time you show me the rest of the house and the movie's over, dinner will be ready. I can wait."

"You wouldn't rather go out?" he asked, turning the knob on the stove.

"And miss your pot roast? Not a chance. Come on. Show me your home." She hooked his arm in hers and tugged him from the kitchen.

The backyard was larger than the front. Michelle pictured a golden retriever romping around a pair of chubby toddlers, a swing set and sandbox under the large weeping willow that aligned with the kitchen window. An unexpected sadness interrupted her fantasy as they walked back inside and climbed the long, winding staircase. It could be so perfect. If only he wanted children.

There it was again. That same old nagging doubt. The vasectomy might have been Jessica's idea, but would he have gone through with it if he truly wanted children? There had to be a way to reconcile these negative facts with her positive feelings. She rubbed her pendant as if it were a good-luck charm, determined to find a way.

Once they were upstairs, Kevin showed her the guest rooms first, then stopped in the doorway of what had to be the master suite. He leaned against the jamb and folded his arms. "Well, this is it. You've seen it all."

Michelle peered past him. A large four-poster bed faced an open-hearth fireplace. Two leather wing-backed chairs flanked a lamp table piled high with medical journals. Unlike the living room, she saw remnants of burned logs in the grate, ashes thick below. Off to one side stood a television console and VCR. Tapes were stacked neatly on top. Michelle slid sideways past Kevin and picked up a few. "Umm ... *Oscilloscope Improvements, Atherosclerosis Update, New Procedures for Vein Grafting ...*"

Kevin sauntered into the room. "Which one do you want to watch?" His smile seared right through her, and she questioned the wisdom of entering his domain.

"I ... I think I saw enough that one day I observed. I don't suppose you have anything a little less gory, like *Interview with the Vampire?*"

He shot her another of those dangerous smiles before he stooped and opened a cabinet door. "Here's one." He held up the tape for her to read.

*"Dances With Wolves."* He wanted her to watch Kevin Costner? Here in his bedroom? After months of total abstinence?

"You don't like it?"

"I love it, but ... well, it's ..." She shrugged. "It's perfect." She sat in one of the chairs and crossed her legs, a trick that had become increasingly difficult with the bulge in her middle.

He eyed her a moment and she wondered if he could see her heart thumping against her sweater. "We don't have to watch it here. We could go downstairs."

She thought a moment. The family room had a big-screen TV, but it also had another unused fireplace and a risky-looking sofa. At least here they'd have separate chairs, and maybe a fire. "Do you have more wood for the fireplace?"

Kevin darted for the door. "Don't move. I'll be right back."

# Thirteen

---

Kevin tried to keep his mind on the movie, but his gaze kept drifting to Michelle's face, and then to her full breasts and rounded tummy. Maybe other men didn't find pregnant women sexy, but that was their loss. He'd seen her in a skimpy bikini when her figure was picture-perfect, but that didn't hold a candle to the beauty she carried now. The sparkle in her eyes, the way her hand absentmindedly trailed over her middle. Her red hair had taken on a new luster, its healthy sheen glowing brighter than the burning embers in front of them. Kevin felt another swelling in his groin and suppressed a groan.

The fire needed more wood. He reined in his traitorous body and pushed out of the chair. He piled three logs at odd angles, stoked the coals below them, then turned around. Michelle's head was lolled to one side, eyes closed, lips slightly parted. Kevin stood with his back to the fire and watched her peaceful face. How had he ever lived in this big, empty house without her? How would he ever again? He worried again about whether he'd have to.

He crossed quietly to her chair, slipping his arms behind her neck and knees and carrying her the short distance to the bed. She made feeble protests but never opened her eyes.

"Sleep for a while, my love. I'll wake you when dinner's ready." She nodded and rolled onto her side facing him, a sweet smile curving her lips ever so slightly. It would be so easy to slip in beside her and never get up. With great restraint, he tiptoed out of the room and walked down the stairs.

He'd known when he brought her here tonight what he would say, what he would ask. The strong aroma of onions greeted him before he entered the kitchen. He checked his watch. About ten o'clock it should be ready. He smiled. It wasn't moonlight, roses and champagne. This probably wasn't how it happened in those romance novels he'd seen her read. He laughed softly as he opened the oven door, a rush of hot air steaming his face as he checked on dinner.

Proposing to a pregnant lover over pot roast. It had to be a first.

All he needed now was a simple yes.

Michelle awoke to the smell of roasting onions and the sight of Kevin bent over the fire probing the coals.

*Ah, a little slice of heaven.* She may have slept through Costner's bare-backside scene, but the view from here seemed infinitely better. She snuggled under the covers, then looked at the comforter. How had she gotten under it? Kevin had carried her to the bed, but beyond that she didn't remember a thing. What an exciting date she'd turned out to be!

Sleep—she couldn't seem to get enough of it lately. Michelle yawned louder than she intended and Kevin turned around.

His gaze was by turns tender and passionate.

"Comfortable?" he asked.

Her heart swelled, leaving her short of breath. "Immeasurably." It was true. She was too comfortable in this man's home, in his bed. A warning signal sounded somewhere in the recesses of her mind, but it wasn't very loud or very insistent.

Michelle held his steady gaze as he moved slowly to the side of the bed. Her mind said she shouldn't, but she knew her eyes telegraphed a different message.

And her eyes didn't lie. There was no point in pretending she didn't want him.

She waited and watched, imagining him shedding his clothes slowly and slipping beneath the sheets beside her. Her imagination was vivid, her memory so clear it might have been yesterday.

To her disappointment, he simply kicked off his shoes and lay on his side atop the covers, propping his head on a bent arm. Fully dressed. Not touching her. Just gazing down at her until all the blood in her body rushed to the most private part of her. Whether it was the fire in the hearth, a hormonal thing or pure lust, she wasn't certain. But she couldn't remember ever feeling this hot.

Ever so gently he lifted a stray lock of hair off her cheek, tucking it behind her ear. Then he raised the pendant from her neck, his gaze drifting from it to her eyes.

"I never thanked you for it, Kevin. I love it. I wear it all..."

His fingers trailed lovingly over her cheek, stopping when they reached her mouth. Her lips parted and he traced the moist inner lining, eliciting moans from deep inside her. She clutched his hand and held it captive, closing her lips around his fingers, her tongue greedy for the taste of him. His eyes closed and his head rocked back, his chest rising and falling faster beneath his starched blue shirt.

She sucked his fingers deeper into her mouth, all the while thinking she'd rip that damn shirt off him, sending buttons flying, if he didn't take it off soon. It, and everything else.

As if reading her mind, he opened his eyes and stared deep into hers.

Quickly Kevin shed the last scrap of clothing and slid naked beneath the covers. Without pausing, he tugged the sweater over her head and tossed her bra on the floor behind him. She helped him tug down her slacks and panties, kicking them to the foot of the bed. Then, finally, he stretched himself alongside her, pressing his long, hard body against hers, flesh to flesh. His arms tightened around her back and he murmured into the hollow of her neck.

"Michelle, Michelle. There hasn't been a night since we met that I haven't thought of this."

He trailed soft, moist kisses down her hot shoulder. She arched a breast to him, wanting the feel of his mouth on her hardened nipple. He cupped her gently, weighing the new heaviness, his eyes full of wonder at the sight of her. The pulsing in her groin begged for relief. She slid lower in the bed, catching his full arousal between her legs, tightened around him like a vise. When his warm mouth suckled her, the first flow of hot liquid rushed from her body and over him. His mouth never leaving her breast, his hips slid back and forth, his sex rubbing her wet and swollen V, again and again, until finally her whole body shuddered against him. Streaks of white light kaleidoscoped behind her closed lids. When he slipped his fingers inside her and stroked faster and deeper, she heard someone scream and felt herself falling into a dark abyss. Desperately she clung to consciousness, pulling Kevin's face to hers. His lips were warm and pliant; hers were hot and needy. She thrust her tongue into his mouth as he thrust himself deep inside her. They swallowed each other's moans of passion and pleasure, their lips pressing harder, their tongues probing deeper.

Kevin rolled onto his back, taking her with him. Michelle sat back on her knees, watching Kevin's dark eyes roll back. His rigid sex pulsed larger inside her as she raised and lowered herself on him, jockeying for the right position, taking the ride of a lifetime. Her stroke grew shorter and faster in pace with his heaving chest, until she knew he was reaching the finish line. She took him fully inside her and lowered her body to him, grinding her hips into him, winding her arms about his back as he arched himself off the bed. He held her tight with an intimacy and need so great she could barely breathe. His spasms traveled the length of him and she held on tight, feeling him spill himself into her.

Their breathing, ragged and loud, slowed in unison. Michelle slumped against him as he sank into the mattress. Eventually he nibbled playfully on her earlobe, his soft chuckle warming her neck.

Michelle pulled her head back and studied his relaxed face. "What's so funny?"

"That wasn't exactly maternal," he said, the corners of his mouth curving upward.

"What's that supposed to mean?" she asked, as if she didn't know.

Kevin sat up and locked his fingers behind her back as she straddled his lap. He leaned forward and kissed her swollen lips tenderly, then smiled. "You shameless hussy."

She slapped at his shoulder and pretended to be offended.

"If that's how pregnant ladies make love, maybe you should have a dozen more."

If only they could, she thought, a wave of sadness bringing her back to reality with a painful thud. She masked her feelings as she usually did, behind a quick smile and clever retort. "So when do we eat? I'm starved."

Kevin shook his head and laughed. "You're insatiable...and so much fun." His expression grew serious and she knew the conversation would, too, if she didn't move that very instant.

She sprang from the bed and headed for the bathroom, snagging his blue shirt off the floor as she went. "I'll give you a hand in the kitchen. Just give me a couple minutes." She shut the door behind her and leaned against it heavily.

*You've really done it this time, Purdue. You know what this night is about. Now what are you going to tell him if he asks?*

There had to be a way. How could she possibly throw away such a kind, loving, handsome—she turned on the hot water and looked into the mirror—and sexy man. God, she did look like a shameless hussy. She laughed aloud. Her bangs were wet and matted to her forehead, and the rest of her hair was a tangled mess.

She washed quickly, her mind racing for a solution. Compromise. How could they compromise without hurting the babies' future? She dried herself and slipped into Kevin's shirt, bringing the collar to her nose—the same musky after-shave she remembered from the cruise. Her thoughts deepened, searching for an answer.

And then one possibility peeked through the darkness. She waited a moment, hoping for another. But nothing else came.

It wasn't the most desirable idea she'd ever come up with, she thought, her hand trailing down the polished banister to the first floor. But for now, it was the only one.


"What do you mean, 'Maybe' and 'We'll have to wait and see'?"

"If it were just the two of us, I'd marry you tonight, Kevin..."

"But?"

"But how do I know how you'll really feel about the babies until I've had time to see you with them? Don't you see? I *chose* to bring them into this world, to love them unconditionally—"

"You don't think I'll be good to your children?" he asked, interrupting her, working to keep his voice even, controlled.

Michelle stared at the wax dripping down the long tapers between them. "Yes. You'll probably be good to my children." She gazed up at him, a pained expression behind her eyes. "But I want more, Kevin. I want someone who will *love* the children, *our* children."

He started to protest, but she held up a hand. "It doesn't matter who the biological father is. A man who truly wants a family would *love* the babies, not just be good to them. He would think of them as *ours*, not mine." Michelle lowered her voice to almost a whisper. "Kevin, I know you love me...and I love you with all my heart. But children were never part of your dream. They were *my* dream."

He poked the last of his roast beef with his fork, then pushed the plate away. It wasn't that he'd never wanted a family. Jessica had never wanted one. Or so she'd said. If he'd been with Michelle all along, they'd probably have a houseful of them by now. Why had he ever agreed to that damn vasectomy?

"I could have it reversed, you know," he said suddenly. She gave him a blank stare. "The vasectomy. There's been success lately in—"

"You'd be doing it for me—"

He raised his voice. "Of course I'd be doing it for you."

"Don't you understand? That's the wrong reason."

*Damn!* He hadn't said that right, either. Nothing was coming out the way he'd planned. He *wanted* children with Michelle. And not just the twins. He was sure he could love them like his own, but one or more who were theirs would be nice, too. He wanted everything life had to offer with this woman. If only she wasn't so stubborn and determined to go it alone.

The defiant tilt of her chin left no doubt that tonight was not the night to push for the answer he wanted. Still, maybe another compromise would work.

"You could live here. There's plenty of room for a nursery and your computer. Then when the babies come, you could see for yourself how well things work."

She held his gaze for the longest time without answering, and for a moment he allowed himself to hope. But then she looked away and he knew he'd deluded himself.

"We can see each other... discreetly. But if I move in here, Kevin—" she looked back at him, her eyes sad and weary "—I'd never want to leave."

*If.* He heard the *if. When* would have felt better. The room took on a sudden chill. The thought of living here without her left him adrift, lonelier than he'd ever felt.

After a strained pause, he asked, "What do you mean, 'discreetly'? Are we supposed to sneak around like a couple of teenagers breaking curfew?" He hadn't meant to sound so sharp, but he was starting to feel angry.

"I've heard enough about the hospital rumor mill to know its leading cardiologist would be chewed up and spit out like sour grapes if he was seen dating a pregnant woman that wasn't his wife," Michelle said, sounding a little angry herself.

"So marry me!" he said, throwing his arms out in exasperation and pushing to his feet.

"We just finished the loop," she said, standing and taking her plate to the kitchen.

Kevin followed her, ignoring the dirty dishes. "I'm not one of your computer glitches, damn it."

Michelle set her dish on the sink and turned to face him. Her eyes were shiny, which made him feel like the jerk he was.

"I'm sorry," he said, wanting to hold her, but afraid she'd pull away.

"So am I," she said after a moment. "It's been a beautiful evening, Kevin—"

He held up a hand, cutting her off. "I'll take you home now, if that's what you want." She nodded, looking at the floor. The air was thick and stifling, as if there weren't enough of it in the room for both of them to breathe.

Kevin paced outside before getting in his car. He sulked behind the wheel, preferring anger to pain. He waited there until she'd dressed and joined him for the silent drive back to the city. And when he dropped her at her door, there were no false promises of "I'll call you later."

"Good night," he said without looking at her. Out of the corner of his eye he could see her fingers on the door handle, lingering, tentative. Then slowly, the door opened.

"Good night, Kevin."

He waited seven agonizing days, believing love and hate were truly the same emotion, until finally, Saturday afternoon, he picked up the phone and dialed. He didn't know what he'd say, but he was tired of feeling like Atlas with the weight of the world on his shoulders.

Michelle answered on the second ring, her voice soft and vulnerable, and Kevin felt his anger fade as he exhaled loudly into the receiver. "I wanted to punish you for shooting me down, but it's not working. I'm the one who's hurting," he said.

"Oh, it's working. I'm miserable."

"I miss you, Purdue."

"I miss you, Singleton."

"Then let's have dinner tonight."

"Some little out-of-the-way place?"

"You name it."

"Anywhere Italian. We're in the mood for lasagna, pizza, spaghetti—"

"Whoa. You can't mean all three."

"No, silly. You order one and I'll order two."

He heard the smile in her voice and his heart was in his throat again. Somehow he had to find the words to convince her she was wrong. They belonged together. Four of them, six of them, it didn't matter how many. "I'll pick you up about six, sooner if I can get away."

"Call me when you're close by. I'll meet you downstairs."

"Don't trust me in your apartment, huh?"

She chuckled into the phone. "No. I don't trust either one of us. Besides, I'm already hungry."

His beeper vibrated on his belt. "Have to run."

"Kevin . . ."

"Yes?"

"I . . . I'm glad—"

Oh, God! She was going to cry.

"Me too, gorgeous. I'll be there as soon as I can."


Michelle slouched in the booth across from Kevin, rubbing her belly and feeling like a stuffed toad. The lasagna hot plate in front of her was empty, and the side of spaghetti they shared had a healthy dent closest to her. She cupped her hand below her breasts defining the tighter space. "Look at that. You can barely tell where one stops and the other starts. I think I've been overdoing my doctor's order to eat more." She stared at herself and rubbed, hoping to generate some activity, though she left them little room to maneuver.

"I think you're beautiful," Kevin said, barely above a whisper.

Michelle gazed up at his loving face. He did think she was beautiful; she could see it in his warm gray eyes. "Beach ball and all?" She had to make light of it or she'd cry. This crying thing happened at the oddest times lately.

"Beach ball and all," he said, reaching across the table for her hand.

The waitress saved her from blubbering into her empty plate. "More wine?" she asked Kevin, raising the bottle in her hand.

Kevin eyed Michelle, then said, "Sure. Just a little." After the glass was replenished, he confessed to Michelle. "On the cruise I wondered if you were a reformed alcoholic."

Michelle started to choke on her ice water, then laughed into her napkin.

"You never had a single drink." He cocked an eyebrow at her. "It never occurred to me you might be pregnant... especially with the body I remember in that skimpy chartreuse thing.''

She laughed again, remembering. ''I was afraid to take my cover-up off in front of you. That had to be the boldest thing I ever wore in public.''

Kevin sat taller, then leaned his elbows on the table and steepled his fingers.

''Oh-oh. Looks serious,'' she said, bracing herself. What controversy had she unearthed now?

''There's a fund-raiser I've been invited to next Saturday night...''

''Kevinnn...'' She strung out his name in warning. He knew how she felt.

He held up both hands in surrender. ''I know, I know. But this is different. It's a costume party... with the proceeds going to the new AIDS hospice.''

That stunned her into thinking a moment. Costumes. A good cause. A night with Kevin. Somewhere in there was a mix that might work. Then she remembered something else.

''Remember Jimmy? The man at my apartment that night you barged in?'' Kevin crossed his arms and leaned back, pretending to be jealous, when she knew very well he remembered the rest—that she'd told him Jimmy was a client who happened to be gay. ''Well, anyway, he sent me an invitation to the same party. I was thinking of going, but how could I with you? If you show up with a pregnant date, everyone will assume you're the daddy.''

''What's wrong with that?''

''If you're the daddy, why haven't you married me and made an honest woman of me?''

''Because you turned me down,'' he said with a wry smile.

''But no one knows that.''

''Yes, they do. I told Paul.''

She stared at Kevin, openmouthed. Maybe she should be angry, but instead it touched her that he had shared such intimate details with his friend. But which details? That he had proposed? That she was pregnant? She shook her head. Right now it didn't matter.

''Don't worry. He won't tell a soul.''

"We're straying from the subject." Michelle leaned forward and rubbed the small of her aching back. "The point is, the gossip will spread like wildfire. And you'll be the heavy. It could hurt your work, your reputation." She knew she didn't sound very convincing. Probably because she wanted to go, she wanted to be talked into it. Kevin saw her waver and pounced on her hesitation.

"There has to be a costume that could conceal your condition, if that's all you're worried about."

"Like what?" she asked, her mind racing, knowing she'd already lost the battle.

"You're creative. You'll think of something."

She sat quietly, trying not to show the excitement that was building inside her, an idea already taking shape in her mind's eye.

"So you'll go?" he asked with a smug smile.

"Maybe. Let me give it some thought. It does sound like fun." She'd need lots of wire, Velcro and, of course, yards of material. And tights. Did they make maternity tights?

"I can see those wheels turning. What's your idea?"

"Sorry, sweetheart. You'll just have to wait and see."

# Fourteen

"Heh, heh, heh." Harry shook his head and laughed his deep, husky laugh. "If ya hadn't talked to me, Ms. Purdue, I'd a never known who ya was. How ya gonna sit down in that thing?"

Michelle turned around and pointed to the center seam. "It's Velcro. I can spin the thing around and open and close it anytime I want." She took off the brown papier-mâché stem and inhaled deeply. "I hope it's cool at the party. This thing is roasting my head."

"Heh, heh, heh. I bet it is. Where'd ya get that pumpkin, anyway?"

Michelle lifted her chin, feeling quite proud of herself. "I made it."

"Ya can't even tell yer ... well ..."

"Pregnant?" she finished for him. He nodded, looking embarrassed, acting as if he'd overstepped his bounds. She squeezed his arm and smiled up into his tired brown eyes. "It's okay, Harry. I don't care if everybody in this building knows I'm going to have a baby ... two, actually."

"Twins?" His shaggy gray eyebrows shot up.

"Yes, sir, twins." She glanced out the door and saw the slate-gray Volvo before finishing her thought. "It's just that I'm going to this fund-raiser with Dr. Singleton...and I don't want everyone jumping to the wrong conclusion, gossiping...you know."

Harry's eyes widened and he gave a slow, knowing nod of his head. Then he smiled. "If ya don't mind me saying, yer legs look real skinny in those green tights. Ya can't tell anything from what I see."

"Thanks, Harry." Out of the corner of her eye, she saw the car door open. Quickly she positioned her stem back on her shoulders and stood quietly next to Harry.

"Heh, heh, heh," he started again.

"Shhh. Don't give me away. It's Halloween. I could be anyone. Let's see if he figures it out."

Kevin strode in and walked directly to Harry just as a pair of witches stepped out of the elevator and walked between them.

When they passed, Kevin asked, "How are you tonight, Harry?"

"Just fine, just fine. And you, Doctor?"

"Great, except for this costume thing." He held out a large black cape, his arms fully extended. Under it he wore a black turtleneck and black slacks. His face was free of makeup or any revealing adornments.

"Excuse me for asking, but what are ya supposed to be?"

"The easiest thing I could come up with." He slapped the old man's hunched shoulders and laughed. "I left the Darth Vader mask in the car. Kind of hard to drive with the thing."

Kevin turned to the pumpkin standing idly to the side. "We better get going, Michelle." He walked toward the exit. "We have a party to go to."

Outside, she spun the wire-shaped orange fabric to the front and released the seam, not wanting to bend a wire when she sat down. Then she turned it back before crawling into the passenger seat and leaned back with a satisfied smile. They pulled away from the curb and she took her stem off, depositing it on her lap, or what was left of her lap. There seemed to be less and less space between her belly and her knees these days. "Well? What do you think?"

"I knew that creative brain of yours would come up with something." He shot her a wink before returning his attention to the road.

"But how could you tell it was me?" She'd taken great pains in placing strategic slits near her eyes, nose and mouth, blending and shading the browns to conceal the small openings. Not only could no one see her bulging middle, they couldn't see her face, either.

"The legs. I'd know those legs anywhere." He kept his eyes on the highway, but she saw the corners of his mouth curve upward ever so slightly.

She knew what he was thinking—the various angles and positions he'd seen those same legs in. If he wasn't thinking that, *she* was, making her skin damp beneath her costume. This thing was hot enough without such thoughts, she told herself as they covered the short distance to the Grosse Pointe War Memorial, where the party was already in full swing.

Michelle watched with amusement as scarecrows, witches and goblins made their way to the entrance. She inhaled one last breath of fresh air, then slid her stem into place, aligning the holes just right, settling the high points of the base over her shoulders. "Wait," she said as they neared the valet. She scooted forward on the seat and faced the side window. "Could you fix the Velcro in the back?" The small interior of the car left her little space to maneuver. Her stem hit the ceiling, forcing her to hunch over.

Kevin stopped the car and pressed the orange pieces together just as the valet opened her door. With his Vader mask firmly in place, they headed for the door, and a moment later they found the darkly decorated ballroom. Faux cobwebs hung from dimmed chandeliers and every other available surface, casting an eerie yet fun atmosphere over the elbow-to-elbow crowd. Over the din came appropriate scary sounds from concealed speakers.

Michelle hooked her arm in Kevin's and giggled, feeling like a little girl about to go trick-or-treating. She couldn't remember the last time she'd been to a costume party. The excitement built with each passing guest. Some said hello, while others simply nodded, presumably not wanting to give away their identities.

"Oh, Kevin. This is so much fun."

"Yeah, right."

In typical male fashion, he tried to sound like the whole thing was dumb and boring, but she knew him too well. The money was going to a good cause and they were together . . . in public, no less.

Kevin elbowed her in the side, sending her pumpkin askew. "Isn't that fairy your friend?" He pointed with the top of his shiny black mask.

Michelle scanned the many faces in the general vicinity of the nod until she spotted Jimmy's face in the crowd. Furious, she swirled on Kevin, fists in the area of her hips. "Kevin! I never would have taken you for a name-calling bigot. Jimmy isn't just a client. He's my friend and I won't have you—" She felt a tap on her shoulder and turned abruptly.

"Michelle? Is that you in there?" Jimmy asked.

She'd told him what she'd be wearing so that he could find her tonight, but he'd never mentioned his costume. She laughed softly behind the stem, glad neither he nor Kevin could see the blush on her cheeks. "You've got the right pumpkin," she said, swallowing another laugh.

Jimmy tapped the top of her stem with the gold star that rested at the end of his long, glittery magic wand. "Nice job," he said, eyeing Michelle from head to toe. Then, done with his inspection, he pirouetted in front of her, his full-skirted lacy white gown billowing out around him. His long blond curls bounced in place.

"Aren't I a vision?" He laughed at himself, looking as though a long-awaited fantasy had been fulfilled. "In fact, you could borrow this little number anytime you want. A tuck here and there and voilà! a wedding dress."

Again, Michelle was grateful her face was hidden. She cleared her throat and turned sideways to include Kevin. "You remember Dr. Singleton? He stopped over once when you were at my apartment."

"Yes, yes...of course." Jimmy gave Kevin's extended hand a gentle squeeze.

A voice behind them called out, "Oh, Jimmy...could I speak with you a moment?"

"See you two later," Jimmy said, winking before he took the arm of a six-foot male ballerina in a pink tutu.

Michelle snuggled as close to Kevin as she could and whispered toward his ear. "Sorry, I thought..."

"Forget it," he said. They faced each other, neither able to see the other's expression. Then she giggled and Kevin let out a laugh, his mask puffing outward. They continued to laugh as hand in hand they weaved their way through the noisy crowd.

Dr. Westerfield, dressed as King Arthur, waved and nudged his way closer.

"Paul, you look terrific!" Kevin said when his friend reached them. "Your wife must have dressed you." The pair laughed and shook hands while Michelle stayed in the background. The last time she'd seen this man, she and Kevin had used his office to argue. This face covering, as hot as it may be, was coming in handy tonight. She didn't have to hide her embarrassed expression when Paul picked up her hand and cupped it between both of his.

"It's nice seeing you again, Michelle...though *seeing you* seems hardly the right phrase. Anyway, I'm glad you got this stuffed shirt to come. He never makes time for fun...or at least he never used to." He slanted a wry grin in Kevin's direction, leaving little doubt in Michelle's mind that the two shared many a confidence.

"Actually," she began, "it was Kevin who talked me into coming."

"Really," Paul said, not very good at feigning surprise.

They'd obviously talked, she thought, or how else would he have known to look for Darth Vader. But did he know she was pregnant? That Kevin wasn't the father? Probably. But, as closemouthed as Kevin was, if he told Paul, the secret had to be safe. Besides, she liked this man. He had a warm sincerity about him that she imagined went a long way as the chief of staff.

"There are a couple large punch bowls behind me, if either of you are thirsty." He gave the pair a curious glance. "Can you get straws in those things?"

They both nodded and pointed at the same time, laughing along with Paul as he stepped between them and led the way.

"The bowl on the left is nonalcoholic," Paul said matter-of-factly.

Well, one question was answered. He knew she was pregnant.

Paul poured her a cup and inserted a straw before handing it to her.

"Thank you," she said, taking a long, cooling pull from the straw.

"Where's your better half?" Kevin asked, scanning the area around them.

"She's at the pledge table, where else?" Paul said, sounding proud. "Near the door." he nodded, his crown shifting slightly on his thick salt-and-pepper hair. "The Queen of Hearts . . . organizing things, twisting arms."

Michelle followed their gazes, finding the tall, attractive woman in red. She was smiling graciously, accepting an envelope from a dragon. Michelle had already given her donation to the hospice, providing hours of free time setting up their computer, installing and teaching various programs. But now she wished she'd done more, that she'd brought a check, too. She sipped punch and thought about what else she could do to help, until an unexpected kick drew her focus inward. She stood very still, smiling behind her mask, waiting for a little elbow or fist to remind her again what hid behind her pumpkin. But when the next blow came, she lost her balance, stumbling awkwardly into Kevin's side, the heat suddenly oppressive.

Kevin stopped talking with Paul and wound an arm around her shoulder. "Are you all right, sweetheart?"

She didn't know. She inhaled as much air as was possible through the narrow slit and braced herself against Kevin. The pressure at the bottom of her belly was growing by the second. It felt as though she were carrying a large sack of potatoes upside down and the opening was about to burst. "May-maybe I should—" A sharp pain ripped through her and she fell to her knees, clutching at Kevin's cape on the way down.

In a heartbeat, Kevin knelt beside her, drawing her closer.

"Can't . . . can't breathe," she managed, clinging to a sliver of light.

Kevin tugged the stem from her head and tossed it aside. Paul asked the curious to step back, which they did, giving Michelle the air she needed. Her eyes opened halfway, sending him a silent thank-you.

"Michelle," Kevin said, cupping her face gently between his long, graceful fingers. "Talk to me. Is it just the heat? Are you in pain?"

Another pain stabbed her harder than the first as she slapped her palms on the parquet floor. She was on all fours now, panting like an overheated dog. She knew the crowd around them had grown quiet. All eyes had to be on her. But she couldn't worry about how she looked. Her only worry was the source of the pain.

"Pain," she whispered between pants, then sat back on her feet and gazed up at Kevin, tears flooding her field of vision. "It's too soon," she said as Kevin tore open her pumpkin and flung it in the direction of the stem. She sat cross-legged now, cradling her big belly, feeling like a giant turtle without its shell.

Kevin stared at the dark stain between her legs. "Do you think you're bleeding?"

Michelle nodded, trying unsuccessfully to stem the flow of tears.

Paul hunkered down in front of them. "I've got the van tonight." Gripping Kevin's shoulder, he said, "I'll drive. You get in the back with Michelle."

Kevin nodded, looking as frightened as Michelle felt, leaving her no doubt her suspicions were right. She was in labor. She slumped more heavily against Kevin, crying softly into his chest. "They're too small." She choked the words out. Kevin stroked her hair and shushed her, whispering words of reassurance she knew he didn't believe.

Paul pointed to a pair of stocky men dressed as Detroit Lions, shoulder pads and all. "You and you. Each take a thigh.

Gently. On the count of three, lift." Paul moved quickly to
Michelle's side, opposite Kevin. "One. Two. Three."

Michelle felt as if she'd been levitated by a magician as she
floated out the door and into the waiting van. Paul tore off
Kevin's cape and stuffed it below her butt. "Keep your head
down and your hips up, Michelle. We'll be at the hospital
soon."

Paul had run as many red lights as was safe, the speedome-
ter doubling the legal limit. He'd already called Michelle's ob-
stetrician on his cellular phone, alerting him of the situation.
Now all they could do was wait.

Kevin glanced over the seat, gauging the time left until they
reached the hospital. Michelle lay perfectly still, her eyes closed,
but Kevin knew she wasn't asleep. He wondered if she was
praying as hard as he was. Nothing could happen to these babies. They had to live and be healthy. He couldn't imagine
Michelle's heartbreak if that wasn't the case.

Kevin's chest constricted and he felt a knot of emotion
choking off his air. If there had been any doubt how he felt
about these babies before, it had just vanished. A long, slow
breath passed over his dry lips. Michelle would not be the only
one to grieve if—

*No!* He shook away the morbid cloud that hung over him
and rested a protective hand on her hard belly.

*Please, God. Just a little longer. I'll be the best father they
could ever have. It doesn't matter whose they are....*

He spotted the emergency entrance and sighed in relief.
"We're here, Michelle."

She opened her sad eyes and gazed at him anxiously.

"It's going to be all right. I promise." A faint smile curved
his lips as he did his best to put her at ease.

A nurse came out with a wheelchair, but Paul motioned her
back. "We need a gurney. She has to stay flat."

Paul came around to the passenger side. "I'll go find her
OB...let him know we're here." With one last penetrating stare
at Kevin, he raced through the automated doors as a pair of
able-bodied men flew by him with the gurney.

Reluctantly Kevin stepped aside and let the attendants do their job, feeling powerless, useless. With all his training and years of dealing with life and death, nothing prepared him for the panic he felt this very moment.

They rode the elevator to the fifth-floor labor and delivery with Kevin holding Michelle's hand, his gaze locked on her worried face. A few minutes later he watched monitors being attached to the three most important people in his life. Then Michelle's OB sailed into the room and a wave of relief passed over her ashen face.

"When did the contractions start, Michelle?" He ignored everything and everyone else in the room, including Kevin, focusing instead on his patient.

Kevin listened as Michelle explained the night's events, feeling like the outsider he was. Not only wasn't he the babies' father, he wasn't the husband or even the fiancé. He knew that before long he'd be asked to leave the room, so he spared himself the embarrassment.

"I'll be right outside, sweetheart. Let me take care of your insurance and a few things while your doctor examines you, okay?" She nodded weakly. He kissed her damp forehead and brushed back a few stray curls, then left before she could see the moisture in his eyes.

He was no sooner out of the room than Paul handed him a cup of coffee and ordered him to sit down. "I did some quick calculating on the drive over. From what you told me, she should be about twenty-eight weeks."

Kevin leaned his head back against the concrete wall and sighed. "Is that long enough?"

"I talked to Lisa in Neonatal ICU. She says ninety-some percent are okay after twenty-six weeks. Twins could be a little different, but not much."

"This Lisa . . . doctor or nurse?" Kevin asked, his voice flat, his head still pressed against the wall.

"A nurse. She's been doing this for fourteen years. We both should realize by now that nurses know better than any doctor."

Kevin rolled his head and eyed Paul. Then they both laughed. "Yeah, you're right. Scary, isn't it?" Kevin allowed himself a moment of optimism and took a long draw on his coffee. "God, Paul. Where'd you get this stuff? It tastes like the scorched bottom of yesterday's pot."

Paul patted him on the shoulder and laughed again. "Glad you're feeling better, Papa."

Kevin's expression sobered. "It's not a sure thing, my friend. You know I've asked her once and where did that get me?"

Paul hunched forward, rested his forearms on his knees and shot Kevin a sly grin. "Yeah, but that was before. She's more vulnerable now."

"Since when have you become so diabolical?" Kevin grinned back.

"Since I saw the way you two looked at each other once those masks came off tonight. I knew how you felt before, but now I know how she feels."

Kevin shook his head. "The fact that she loves me is not in dispute. It's the babies. She doesn't think I want children."

"Gee...wonder if telling her about your vasectomy had anything to do with that?" Kevin's head dropped between his shoulders and Paul changed tactics. "Have you thought about talking to the guy who snipped you? Ask about a repair job?"

Tired of sitting, Kevin shot out of the chair, tossed away the dregs of his coffee, then paced the hall a couple of times before stopping in front of Paul. "If I can find him this weekend, I'll talk to him. If not, first thing Monday I'll give his office a call. It's worth a shot."

The OB walked out of Michelle's room, looking tired, the way all OBs looked, but not disheartened. He walked to Kevin and Paul and shook hands as Paul made the introductions.

"Larry Wilson...Kevin Singleton. Kevin's in cardiology here."

Larry dropped in a chair beside Kevin. "We got monitors on Michelle and the babies. No sign of fetal distress."

Kevin exhaled loudly.

"But she was almost two centimeters dilated, so I ordered Terbutaline to stop the labor. We've started an IV and sent cultures to the lab to rule out infection. She's resting comfortably at the moment...all things considered."

He looked away and Kevin read the body language. Something else was wrong. "And?"

"And I discovered an incompetent cervix. Earlier in the pregnancy I would have stitched her, but at this late date and with the added weight of twins, well..." He folded his arms across his chest and eyed Kevin, as if trying to assess his exact role in all this. Then he added, "Michelle said to talk to you, but since you're not her husband, fiancé or relative, you can understand my reluctance in discussing the particulars of her case."

"I'm also a doctor on staff at this hospital who can find out whatever he damn well wants if you don't tell me," Kevin shot back, taking an aggressive stance.

Paul intervened. "Back off, Kevin. The guy's just doing his job." Paul turned to the OB. "Look, Larry, I don't see any need to beat around the bush here. Kevin and I both know Michelle was artificially inseminated, which means we all know Kevin's not the father. But what you don't know is that since that time these two people have developed a very important relationship. If Michelle wants you to discuss her case with Kevin, trust me. It's okay."

Kevin sat back and exhaled. "I apologize, Larry. I should know better. I forgot for a second I was a doctor, too."

"That's a hopeful sign," Paul said, slapping him on the shoulder with a relieved chuckle.

Larry heaved a sigh and continued. "Okay. The situation is this. With luck, the Terbutaline will do the trick for now and stop the labor. But the only solution for incompetent cervix is total bed rest until delivery...which we hope to hold off as long as possible. Michelle's not going to like it much, but I've ordered the bed to stay in Trendelenberg for now."

Kevin smiled at long last. "Having her head pointed to the floor will probably be the least of her complaints. She'll want to go home."

Larry smiled back. "She's already asked when she can. And you're right—she didn't like my answer. But I explained the risks and it seemed to quiet her. She wants those babies. Real bad."

Kevin swallowed hard before he asked the next question. "So what's your prognosis, Doctor?"

"The babies seem okay for now and they're developed enough to survive outside the womb, but they'd be very small...which would mean months of incubation. Michelle would have to go home without them. No new mother likes that." He leveled his unruly eyebrows on Kevin. "If you can convince her to stay here the duration...and relax—" he leaned heavily on the last word "—then she has a better than fifty-fifty chance of carrying those babies till they're at least four-plus pounds, which means if there are no other complications, they might be able to go home with Mama...or soon after."

Kevin puffed out his cheeks and exhaled toward the ceiling. Then he grabbed the OB's hand and pumped it firmly. "She'll stay if I have to tie her down and gag her. Thanks, Larry." He looked anxiously at Michelle's door.

"You can go in for a while, but she's pretty groggy."

Kevin didn't wait for a second invitation.

# Fifteen

---

**T**hree weeks of blood rushing to her head did little to improve Michelle's disposition. Kevin slept every night at the hospital, occasionally running home for clothes and mail before rushing back. Between surgeries and catnaps, or when sleep failed him at odd hours of the night, he found himself at Michelle's bedside. Sometimes they'd just hold hands and nod off together. At others they'd talk, filling in the gaps in each other's lives before the cruise: *b.c.*, as it had come to be called.

But this afternoon Michelle was in a quarrelsome mood, one that had become more common of late.

"My head is pounding. I feel like a prizefighter going down for the final count. Can't you talk someone into letting me lie *level* at least?"

"I'm not your doctor, sweetheart. Have you—"

"Yes, yes. I asked my doctor. A lot of good that did."

Kevin pressed his lips to her hand. She glared at him and turned away. Then slowly she looked back, her eyes shiny. "I'm sorry. This must be hell for you, too. When was the last time you got a good night's sleep?"

"The same night as you—before Halloween." He trailed his hand up and down her arm, reassuring her it didn't matter. "Look at it this way. We've learned about each other during this time . . . time we would have spent doing something else." Instead of cheering her, that opened the floodgates.

"How can you even look at me?" she asked between sobs. "My hair is a tangled mess . . . no makeup . . . this ugly hospital gown. I look like a beached whale with my head buried in the sand." Kevin handed her another tissue and she gave a resounding blow. "This isn't at all like my romance novels." She blew again, then dabbed at her eyes with a dry corner.

When it looked as if her latest wave of emotion had subsided, Kevin decided a change of subject might help. Risky as the subject was, he'd rather see her angry than crying. "I went to see an urologist today."

She looked at him suspiciously. "About me?"

He fidgeted, smoothing her sheets. "No."

"Kevin. You're not sick, are you?"

He met her worried eyes and squeezed her hand. "No. I'm healthy as a horse. I wanted to ask him a few questions . . ."

"About . . ." she pushed, impatience seeping into her weary voice.

"About reversing my vasectomy," he said quickly, before she could cut him off again.

"I thought we had this talk. Doing this for me isn't—"

This time Kevin interrupted. "I'm doing this for me . . . for us. After what you're going through now, maybe you won't want more children. But if you do, so do I . . . as long as they're with you." She started to speak, but he held a finger to her lips. "I love you, Michelle." He placed his free hand on her ever-ballooning belly. "And I love these babies as if they were my own." He saw her eyes glaze over again and he attempted a lighter mood. "After all, I've been with them almost since day one. What other man can say that, hmm?"

Michelle bit her bottom lip and shook her head. "None."

"Then it's settled. I have a break in my schedule Friday afternoon. I'll try to get it done then." He leaned back in his chair, relieved that the decision had been made, and even more relieved that she seemed to accept it. Progress. He'd take every inch he could get. He flashed her a devilish smile. "So . . . will you sign my cast?"

It took a couple of beats, but then she laughed, grabbing the bottom of her belly with both hands. "Stop it," she said between giggles. "You're going to make me wet my pants."

"I didn't know you were wearing any." He laughed at her laughing, a larger-than-life love filling him to overflowing.

"I'm not. So please . . . really. You can't make me laugh. Water runs downhill, you know?"

Kevin laughed louder, ignoring her plea. Finally he stood and pressed her damp cheek to his. "I'll show you a little mercy and go back to work." He kissed her warm lips, lingering there longer than he intended. Michelle parted his lips with her tongue and he took her inside him with a moan. Suddenly he pulled back, catching her lascivious grin. "You're not as sick as you look, Ms. Purdue."

"Come back when you have more time and we'll explore that subject."

She raised and lowered her eyebrows a few times in rapid succession as he waved a behave-yourself finger at her and left the room.

Kevin checked his watch. With an hour to spare before his next surgery, he headed straight for the urologist's office in the wing adjacent to the hospital. The sooner he got it over with, the better. Just because there wasn't a cast didn't mean it didn't hurt like hell. He hoped they could squeeze him in Friday. That would leave him the weekend to stay off his feet. He'd get someone else to cover emergencies.

A few minutes later, waiting in an examining room, he wondered if maybe he should get someone to cover part of the following week, too. The doctor entered the room studying Kevin's old chart, a frown on his already heavily lined face.

The old man dropped into the chair near the door and eyed Kevin over his wire-rimmed glasses. "You never came back after the surgery."

It was more an accusation than a question. No, he hadn't. There'd been no need. At first he'd never seemed to find the time. Then when Jessica made her little announcement and moved out, it had seemed a moot point. Besides, vasectomies almost always worked.

Kevin spared the old man his sad story. "I plan to marry soon," he started, wondering what Michelle would say about his choice of words. "Things are different in my life now and I was hoping you could reverse my rather hasty decision."

"How do we know there's anything to reverse?"

Kevin stared at him, his mouth dropping open. The thought had never crossed his mind. "Well, I just assumed—"

The old man smiled, then with shaky fingers handed him a cup. "You know the drill, Doctor. Take as long as you need." He started to leave.

"Surely you don't mean . . ."

He smiled broadly, exposing a perfect set of dentures. "Surely I do. I'm leaving for the day. So call me tomorrow and I'll give you the results." And with that he closed the door between them and left Kevin to his mission.

With surgery and rounds completed, Kevin slowed his pace as he neared Michelle's room. A part of him wanted to tell her about his appointment and the excitement he'd felt all afternoon, but it was premature. Not having had the follow-up exam years ago was one thing; having live sperm now was another. Besides, whatever the results, this had nothing to do with the twins. They'd used protection every time. The future was what excited him, not to mention the fact that he might be spared the uncomfortable procedure come Friday afternoon.

By the time he entered Michelle's room, he'd decided to steer clear of the subject all together. There was another subject needing attention. With newfound energy, he bounded across the room and dropped a quick, noisy kiss on her pale cheek. She barely acknowledged his arrival, grunting a syllable or two and motioning him to sit down. Her eyes were riveted on the video playing on the opposite side of the bed. Finally she hit the pause button and turned to him.

"The nurse brought me this Lamaze tape, since we won't be able to attend classes."

*We?* This was a good sign.

"Do you know how to do this?" she asked, flushed with excitement.

"No. I'm afraid it wasn't part of my training. But I'm not too old to learn."

"I never asked you if you'd be my coach." She lowered her lashes, looking a little embarrassed.

He took the remote control from her hand and pressed rewind. "I'd be mad as hell if you asked anyone else." He winked at her, hoping she wouldn't cry again. God! How he hated to see her cry. It tore at his gut and made him feel so helpless. "Have you learned anything from the tape yet?"

"Sure! How does this sound?" She pushed out her lips as if blowing out candles. "Whoo whoo whoo. And then later comes hee hee hee." She slanted him a sly smile. "Pretty sexy stuff, huh?"

Perfect. She was in a playful mood. Maybe tonight . . .

"I got another video when we're done with this one." She waved it at him, then set it back down on the bed. "It's on twins . . . everything you ever wanted to know and more."

"Now there's a subject I'm familiar with."

"I would think so. Biology, anatomy, whatever."

"More than that." He sat back in the side chair, an eerie, unidentifiable feeling creeping over him. He'd never told her. The subject had never come up.

"Kevin? Is something wrong?"

His gaze locked on hers, a piece of some strange puzzle taking form. He wanted to dismiss this sudden notion, but it was magnifying and multiplying out of control.

"Kevin?"

He blinked and the image cleared. "I'm sorry," he said, pulling himself back. "Where were we?"

"Did something bad happen in surgery today?" She squeezed his hand, and he saw the worry etched in her forehead.

"No. No. I just drifted off there for a while. Guess I'm more tired than I thought."

"We can watch videos another time," she offered gently.

"Do you mind?" In truth, he knew his concentration wouldn't be on the screen.

"I have all day or night to watch it. It can wait."

Even in this position, he thought she was beautiful. She had more heart and soul than anyone he'd ever met. The reality of that pure fact freed him to say the words he'd wanted to say for weeks. He set the remote aside and took both her hands in his, his gaze steady, his voice thick with emotion.

"Will you marry me, Michelle?"

She met his gaze evenly, looking deep into his soul. He showed her everything he had to offer. No words could express the way he felt about this woman. He hoped she could see his love and feel it through his fingers as he held her close to his heart, without words, without moving.

Her answer was slow in coming, but he'd sit there for hours, looking her in the eye all night if that was what it took. He loved all three of them. She had to see it. She had to feel it.

There was only one word that he wanted to hear, that he could bear to hear.

Tears started trickling down the sides of her eyes and onto the pillow, but there was no smile on her face. For a fleeting moment, he thought he'd lost her again. He lowered his gaze to her hands, not wanting to watch her lips when they formed the wrong word.

Then she squeezed his fingers. Tight.

"Yes."

His head snapped up in time for him to see the corners of her mouth quiver into a tentative smile. "Yes?" He asked, not trusting his own ears.

"Yes," she said louder, nodding her head, a fresh flow of tears soaking her pillow.

Struggling with the odd incline, Kevin eased himself onto the bed beside her and gently slipped his arm beneath her head. He kissed the top of her hair and massaged her belly, feeling as though his heart would burst through his chest.

Michelle snuggled closer. "This better not be part of your bedside manner with other patients," she teased, her voice low and husky.

"You're not my patient. You *try* my patience sometimes. But you're not my patient," he repeated, digging deep into his reserve of emotional control. His heart was beating so fast it hurt, which left him worrying how Michelle was coping with all this. She was supposed to remain calm, relaxed. He wasn't contributing to the effort.

After a long pause, she whispered, "What are you thinking?"

"How very much I love all of you . . . how complete I feel."

She brushed a light kiss along his neck. "Anything else?"

He held her away from him and eyed her. "Is there something else I'm supposed to say?" He smiled down at her glossy green eyes, determined to keep things light, for her sake if not his own.

"Earlier I had a feeling there was something on your mind that you weren't telling me," she said, studying his face.

There was. But it would have to keep. "Well, now that you ask—"

She poked him in the ribs with an elbow. "I knew it."

Kevin played along, rolling his eyes to the ceiling, looking for all the world as if he were about to reveal some innermost secret.

"What? What?" she prodded impatiently.

"I was just thinking how uncomfortable this Trendelenberg position is. I think I'd better go find Larry and see if we can't raise this thing to at least level."

Michelle crossed her arms under her breasts and heaved a sigh. "Men."

An hour later, with the mattress parallel to the floor, Michelle watched Kevin pace the foot of the bed and she giggled. "You're making me dizzy. Hold still."

"There's so much to do and so little time," he said, ignoring her request.

They'd agreed on next Thursday, Thanksgiving Day, for the big event, thinking it very appropriate. She'd have married him tonight if it was possible. But there was the matter of a license and the mandatory three-day wait.

"I could get the hospital chaplain," he said, stopping in midstride. "Or do you want me to contact someone else?"

"The chaplain will do fine," she said, wondering which of them was more excited. Until now, she'd thought only women got excited about weddings. She smiled at his intense concentration, loving him all the more for it.

"I'll need some papers from your apartment so I can apply for the license. Maybe I should go and get them now. I'll be in surgery all morning."

"That's a good idea," she said, not wanting him to leave, but exhausted from all the excitement. Quickly she explained where he could find everything, while Kevin found her keys in the bedside drawer. "And while you're there, could you..." She paused and looked away, wishing the subject never had to be mentioned again. But it had to. At least one more time. "In the drawer to the right of my computer is a folder with all the donor information. I don't know if I'll need it for anything, but just in case, would you mind bringing that, too?" She saw a flicker of something pass over his face, but then he smiled.

"Sure. No problem."

"And as long as you're out, why don't you go home and get a good night's sleep?" she said, rubbing her belly. "We'll be okay till morning."

"Trying to get rid of me already?"

"Welll..." She stifled a yawn, teasing him. "We are kind of tired."

"Okay. I can take a hint." He bent over and met her lips with a tender kiss, then gazed into her eyes. "You're off the hook tonight. But tomorrow we work on Lamaze." He rested a possessive hand on her mounded middle. "Never know how soon our babies will decide to arrive."

She didn't miss his use of the word *our*. She pulled his face back to hers and gave him a big, sloppy kiss. "It's a deal, Doctor."

Michelle watched him leave, thinking she had to be the happiest and luckiest woman on the face of the earth.

If only she had someone to share her good news.

Mom and Dad would've adored Kevin. And the babies... they would have spoiled them rotten. She closed her eyes and tried to sleep, feeling the toll of the past few hours. The bed was more comfortable now that the head had been raised, but sleep was still impossible.

What would she wear? Certainly not this skimpy hospital gown. And it would be nice if someone could help her with her hair. Nurses had been rolling her into the shower room, where she used the flexible nozzle to bathe and shampoo. But a wedding called for more.

And rings. Kevin would need a ring. It didn't seem right that he'd have to buy his own.

Michelle gazed out the window at the cloudless dark sky. A thousand diamond-bright stars winked back at her. She'd always pretended two of them were her parents watching over her. She picked a pair shining brightly and close together and stared at them a moment, until a slow smile tugged at the corners of her mouth.

"Yes!" she said aloud. "Why didn't I think of them earlier?"

Kevin left Recovery at lunchtime the next day, his mind still on his patient, running through his checklist one last time. Once he was satisfied that all was in order, his thoughts shifted gears. He wondered if his urologist was out to lunch and if so, whether he might be in the cafeteria or the doctors' lounge.

He found the nearest phone and called the office. The machine was on. He could wait an hour and try again, but his curiosity begged for relief. Michelle cherished his midday visits, but this one would have to wait. Before he talked with her again, he'd have an answer to at least one of the questions that had kept him awake most of the night.

Kevin found the bespectacled old man in the cafeteria, reading the paper by himself near the window. With long strides, Kevin crossed the room and sat down opposite the raised paper, not waiting for an invitation.

The doctor finished what he was reading, then lowered the paper and gazed mischievously over his glasses at Kevin. "Yes?"

"I've been in surgery all morning. This is the first break I've had to find you."

"And that you have." He smiled, stretching the game further than Kevin wanted to.

"So... am I on for surgery tomorrow afternoon?"

The old man took off his glasses and rubbed the bridge of his nose. When the frames were back in place, he smiled and said, "No."

"No?" Maybe the guy's schedule was full. He was afraid to get his hopes up too soon.

"No, Dr. Singleton. There'll be no surgery Friday."

"And exactly why is that?" Kevin didn't mean to sound irritated, but he was.

The doctor leaned across the table and whispered, "Because you have enough live sperm to impregnate the entire nursing staff of this hospital."

Kevin straightened his back, the news sucking the breath from him.

The old man took a drink of water, then added softly, "High count—fast swimmers, too."

Kevin chuckled and shook his head, still not believing his ears. "Thanks, Doc. You've made my day."

"You've made mine," he said, leaning back. "Now I can leave early for up north. Got some fish waiting for me."

Kevin shook the man's hand and pushed out of his chair, barely able to contain himself.

Now how much did he tell Michelle? he asked himself, half walking, half running, down the hall to the elevator. He'd kept three pieces of the puzzle from her, not knowing what, if anything, each meant. Now two pieces were fact. Only one was supposition.

The elevator door slid open and he stepped inside, punching number five. It didn't matter who the father was. She had to believe that. It was *important* to him that she believe that. If he told her what he knew and it proved useless, would she be let down when the babies were born? Maybe. Probably.

The elevator dinged and he stepped out. Did she have a right to know?

Definitely.

Kevin stepped up his pace, eager to share his news before he changed his mind. When he saw that she was alone, he moved quickly to her bedside. Without so much as a hello, he blurted out, "Can you handle more excitement after last night?"

Michelle locked her fingers behind her head as she flashed him a Cheshire cat grin. "Sure. Can you? Wait till you hear." Her hands came down and rubbed her belly.

"Wait till *you* hear," he shot back.

"Really? Okay. You first."

"No. You go first." Kevin pulled up a chair and sat down, leaning his elbows on the edge of the bed. As eager as he was to tell her everything, his news was bound to take time and a great deal of discussion.

"I called Millie and Hazel this morning," she began, then waited for his reaction.

"No! Really?"

Michelle nodded, her smile lighting her beautiful face.

"You told them everything?" he asked, certain he knew the answer.

She averted her gaze. "Well . . . almost everything." After a moment, she looked back at him. "They assumed you're the father...and I let them." Before he could comment, she rushed on. "You will be in every way. I didn't see the need to explain. You don't mind, do you?"

Kevin brought her fingers to his lips and kissed them gently. "No, I don't mind."

Michelle exhaled loudly. "Good. Because they'll be here in a few days and I didn't—"

"Whoa. They're coming here?" Kevin didn't suppress his surprise or his delight. Millie and Hazel. He could picture them fussing already, their frail little fingers busier than at a women's quilting bee—if there was such a thing anymore.

"Yes! They're coming here. Oh, Kevin. I'm so excited. They said they'd help me with everything—my hair, my clothes, your... Well, everything," she said, hunching up her shoulders, looking like a little girl. "They're even thinking of getting a hotel room and staying till the babies are born."

Kevin saw the moisture in Michelle's eyes and he knew what she was thinking. If her mother couldn't be here, what better grandmothers than Millie and Hazel? This was indeed good news. Now he wondered about his own news. How much more excitement could he expect Michelle to handle? Last night's proposal and the imminent arrival of the sisters might be enough for now. Suddenly he wished he'd thought to discuss this with Paul first, or maybe her doctor...

"Your turn," she said, glowing as only a happily pregnant woman can glow. When he didn't immediately answer, she added, "Can't top my news, can you?" She looked pretty smug, locking her hands behind her head again.

# Sixteen

———

"**Y**ou're what?!" Michelle practically shouted the words.

"Fertile. You know...like in live sperm, capable of procreating—"

"I know what the word means," she said, shooting him a look of exasperation. "But how could that be?"

"Sometimes the surgery isn't successful, sometimes the body repairs itself." He shrugged his indifference, feeling a little smug himself, now that he'd started.

"I haven't talked with Dr. Wilson about more children," she said pensively, her sudden joy at hearing the news fading visibly.

"It doesn't matter whether we have more," Kevin said, rocking back in his chair.

"It may have taken me a while to realize it, but I know you'll love the twins as if they're your blood. But you'll want your own, too. Won't you?"

Her eyes begged for reassurance, and he would give it to her. But in proper order. "Speaking of blood...the folder you asked me to get is in my briefcase. I'll bring it by later."

"What's that got to do with blood?"

"I knew you wouldn't mind, so I checked the donor's blood type noted on the forms."

"And?"

"It's A negative."

"I know. So is mine. That's one of the reasons I picked that one." Michelle looked at him from the side of her face. "What's this leading to, Kevin?"

"The twins will have to test A negative . . ."

"Yes, yes. So?"

". . . if they're the donor's babies."

Kevin watched her expression turn from confusion to awareness, then back to confusion. "My type is B negative," he explained. "If the babies are AB negative or B negative, then they can't possibly be the donor's."

Michelle hunched up on her elbows, eyes widening. "But Kevin, how could it be? I mean . . . well, we used protection the entire cruise."

Kevin stood and eased Michelle's shoulders back onto the mattress. "I know. That's what kept me awake all night thinking. But then it came to me. Remember the very first time?"

"Of course I do." She smiled up at him. "We couldn't wait for dinner to end so we could go back to the room and tear each other's clothes off." She touched his cheek as she spoke, trailing her fingers along his jawline.

Kevin lifted her hand from his face and held it between both of his. "I'm talking about the same night . . . but before dinner. We didn't use anything then, remember?"

Light dawned slowly on her face, but doubt still lingered. "Kevin . . . you never . . . I mean . . . there wasn't . . ." Finally she stopped stammering. "Come on, help me out here."

"Simple. Penetration isn't necessary. Strong swimmers can reach their destination if they're anywhere near it." He smiled a cocky smile. "And guess what my urologist told me today?"

"Strong swimmers?"

"Strong swimmers."

Michelle half laughed, half cried, her arms winding around his neck, pulling him to her. "Oh, Kevin. Could it possibly be true?"

He held her tight, praying to God that it was true, but knowing that in the end it wouldn't truly matter. In his heart these babies were his. Either way. "I'd say there's better than a fifty-fifty chance that they're *not* the donor's."

She pushed him back and looked him in the eye. "Better than fifty-fifty?"

"There's something else you don't know."

Michelle slapped at his shoulder. "Out with it, out with it." She was still laughing or crying—he couldn't tell which.

"My mother was a twin."

The whoop she let out sent a nurse darting around the corner. "Is something wrong?"

Over Kevin's shoulder, Michelle said, "Not a thing. Everything's perfect."

The nurse stood there a moment, uncertain, then turned and left with a shrug.

His back aching from the awkward stoop, Kevin dropped back into the chair, wiping the moisture from his own eyes before handing Michelle the box of tissues.

She blew, then laughed, then blew again. When she stopped, a sudden sadness appeared around her eyes as her smile disappeared. "But what if . . ."

He cut her off, matching her intense tone. "Do you honestly think it will change how I feel?"

She hesitated only a moment. "No."

His voice still stern, he said, "Smart woman."

He held her steady gaze as they sat quietly, absorbing the facts, lost in the dream of a miracle neither had imagined until today. It was some time before either spoke again, each content with the love and hope that flowed through their veins.

Eventually Michelle opened her mouth to speak, then shut it. Kevin saw her mind at work behind narrowed eyes that darted here and there, never focusing or landing on any one spot. Patiently he watched and waited, predicting in his own mind what she would ask.

"Is . . . is there a way to find out before they're born?"

Her logical computerlike brain zeroed right in, almost word for word, and Kevin was ready with the answer.

"Bottom line?"

She nodded.

"No. Drawing blood from either of the babies is too risky. It's only done in extreme cases—never for purposes of determining paternity." He saw her look of disappointment, but pushed on, giving her the rest of the story before she could ask.

"If we'd suspected something earlier—when you had the amniocentesis—DNA tests could have been run for paternity. But it's too late now. The fluid isn't kept." Hoping to put a happier spin on things, he rubbed her shoulder and said, "Let's look at it this way. You didn't want to know the sex of the babies, even though it's in your record. Right?"

She jutted out her chin, looking both brave and vulnerable. "Right."

"So this will be one more surprise we wait for. Even if you go full-term—which we both know isn't likely—we'll know in less than six weeks. Okay?" He lowered his head and raised his eyebrows. "Okay?" he asked again at her level.

She pouted a little, but in the end she said, "Okay. I guess there's not much choice."

Kevin stood and patted her knee. "I wish I didn't have to leave, but one of us has to make a living."

She waved him off with the back of her hand. "Well then, go do it."

Michelle watched him leave, then closed her eyes and blew out a long, slow breath. "Relax," she said aloud, then laughed.

If only she could do a little work to take her mind off things. Soap operas and talk shows had lost their appeal weeks ago. The phone stared at her, challenging her to pick it up. She could call her customers, see how things were going. Jimmy had been kind enough to cancel all her appointments and let them know what had happened. Would there be any business left when she got out of here?

Did she care?

The thought startled her. She'd prided herself on her independence. She loved her work, helping people clear the cobwebs from this new technological age. With Kevin she'd never have to worry about money. And the twins were bound to keep her busy for some time. Still, her brain would atrophy without mental exercise.

She reached for the phone. Courtesy calls could keep her busy for days if she paced herself. Later, when she was ready for work again, if her clients had replaced her, they'd surely refer her to friends. There never seemed to be any shortage of people in need of help when it came to computers.

Between naps, meals, visits with Kevin, the Lamaze tape and client calls, the weekend passed quickly, leaving Michelle exhausted and relieved by the time Millie and Hazel breezed through the door, laden with flowers and stuffed animals. They each took a side of the bed, smothering her with hugs and kisses, chattering simultaneously and making her laugh.

She held one of each of their freckled little hands and smiled up at them. "It's so good to see both of you again. I can't thank you enough for dropping everything and coming here."

"Pshaw," Millie said, waving her free hand. "What could be more exciting than this?"

"Or more romantic?" Hazel added.

Michelle gazed lovingly from one smiling face to the other. Including these warm and wonderful women in the plans was one of the smartest decisions of her life, that and deciding to marry Kevin—which reminded her of something.

"While we're alone, I need to ask a special favor."

"Anything," they said in unison.

"I need a ring for Kevin before Thursday. I can suggest a few places nearby if you don't mind."

"Mind?" Millie said, rolling her eyes. "We'd love to. Buying jewelry is one of our favorite hobbies." Both women held up their hands, reminding her of the many rings and bracelets they wore.

"But how will we know his size?" Hazel asked, her thin, light eyebrows pinching together.

"Remember I told you about his friend Paul?" They nodded vigorously. "I've written out directions so you can find his office downstairs. I'm sure he can help...if you can ever catch up with him. His secretary might have to beep him for you. In the meantime, why don't you both sit down and relax?"

They each pulled up a chair and for once Michelle could look someone straight in the eye without wrenching her neck. "Tell me all about your latest vacation—who you met, what you did, everything."

"We'll have days and days to do that, dear." Millie wiggled her narrow shoulders and took Michelle's hand again.

On her side, Hazel scooted closer and followed suit. "We've been dying to hear how you're going to deliver these babies. Everything's so different since our time."

"Will you be doing that modern thing... Oh, what's it called? Something like one of those Pontiac cars." Frustrated, she glared at her sister for help.

Hazel lifted her chin and proudly supplied the answer. "Le Mans."

Michelle bit her lip to keep from laughing. "I think you mean Lamaze. Yes. I've been watching videos on how to breathe correctly. I can't say I have it mastered, but Kevin will help me when the time comes."

"You're so brave, Michelle," Hazel said. "Does that mean you'll be awake through the whole thing? Even delivery?"

Michelle nodded. "I wouldn't call myself brave, though. Drugs and all those artificial procedures aren't good for the babies." She saw them exchange a worried glance. "Oh, I'm sure it's going to hurt, but if you breathe right, I've been told it eases the pain considerably. And since they'll probably arrive early, the twins will be smaller than most babies, so that should make it easier, too."

They were both avoiding eye contact with her now, eyeing each other instead, and acting as though she'd lost her marbles.

"We can't wait to meet Kevin's friend, Paul," Millie finally said, changing the subject.

Hazel brightened. "Will Paul be the best man?"

"Yes." Just last night she and Kevin had discussed this very subject and come to the same conclusion. "And guess who will stand up for me?" Michelle smiled mischievously, trying to take both of them in with a single glance.

"Who?" Millie asked, not suspecting.

"Both of you," Michelle said, with a rush of happiness and excitement.

"Both?" Hazel asked.

"Why not? The law says you must have two witnesses. It doesn't say you can't have three."

The pair looked at each other in shock, then actually started bouncing up and down, squealing with first laughter then tears.

"Bridesmaids! Who would have ever guessed at our age?" Millie started fanning herself.

"We'll have to get new dresses, sister." Hazel walked over to Millie's side of the bed and hooked her arm. "Should they be matching? Maybe with little veils?" she asked Michelle. Without waiting for an answer she looked at her sister and frowned. "Oh, dear. Matching shoes. There probably isn't time for matching shoes."

Michelle cradled the bottom of her belly with both hands, laughing harder than she could remember doing in months, maybe since the cruise.

Millie turned to Michelle. "And you, dear. We'll have to get you something pretty." She stared at Michelle's big belly. "Hmm . . . Let's see."

"What about a frilly little white bed jacket?" Hazel suggested, sending Michelle into another round of giggles. If this continued much longer, she'd have to ask them to hand her the bedpan.

Suddenly the older women stopped their chatter and eyed Michelle. As usual, Millie took the lead.

"Maybe we should go find Paul now and let you rest. I'm not sure all this excitement is helping you any."

It was helping her mental state, but physically she was exhausted. Besides, she'd rather use the bedpan in private. "I could use a nap."

Millie took Hazel's elbow and ushered her toward the door. "Come on, sister. We have work to do."

They gave Michelle little waves, chest-high, then picked up their running dialogue where they'd left off.

"Flowers," Millie started as she neared the door.

"And streamers," Hazel added. "Oh, oh...and those white crepe-paper bells that you unfold . . . You know the ones. . . ."

Their voices trailed off and Michelle closed her eyes, happy yet spent, and glad for the solitude. A kick to the bladder reminded her of two things—she wasn't truly alone, and she'd better buzz the nurse before she had an accident.

Later, with the help of a couple of pillows, Michelle rolled onto her side and let out a satisfied sigh. Amazing, she thought, how the simple act of rolling over brought such pleasure. During today's visit, Dr. Wilson had told her she could start moving. In fact, it helped the babies' oxygen, he said. He also said the babies had dropped into position, which meant she'd probably be home for Christmas. He assured her all was going well and that the steroid shots he'd ordered would help the babies mature faster, though weight should no longer be a problem.

Michelle arched her back and massaged her tailbone with her fingers. She'd thought getting off it for a while would relieve the pressure, but for some reason it felt worse. And as the week progressed, so did the intensity and frequency of the pains in her lower back.

When Kevin sat beside her late Wednesday night after rounds, she let out a groan and he jumped to his feet. "What's wrong?" he asked, his voice full of anxiety.

"I'm pregnant," she snapped, not meaning to sound so cross. "I'm sorry," she said, stealing a glimpse at his worried dark eyes. "I can't get comfortable anymore. I've spent too much time on my back and I must weigh a ton. Rolling over is an aerobic workout."

He sat back down and flashed her a teasing grin. "You sure it's not the idea of getting married tomorrow that's making you irritable?"

"What do you mean, irritable?" she shot back.

"Excuse me," he said, still grinning. "I meant to say uncomfortable."

"I'm certain," she said firmly, not in the mood for games. "I'm certain I want to marry you. I'm certain I want to have these babies. I'm certain I want to get out of this damn bed and go home." Her voice grew louder with each certainty.

"Good." Kevin nodded tolerantly. "I'm glad to hear that." Then turning his head away, he said under his breath, "As is everyone else on the floor."

"I heard that!" Michelle said between clenched teeth.

"And so did we," Millie said, tottering into the room, Hazel right behind her, each loaded down with more packages. "Now, now, you two. Kiss and make up." She set the purchases aside with the other boxes and bags. "Tomorrow's a very special day and we want you both to enjoy it."

Michelle rolled her eyes to the ceiling. Even Millie and Hazel were getting on her nerves. She knew they meant well, but the streamers hanging from the suspended ceiling, with little white bells at each grid crossing were making her crazy. Still, she gave Kevin a perfunctory kiss on the nose when he leaned over the bed.

"There. That's better," Millie said.

Hazel elbowed her in the side. "Maybe we should go back to our hotel, Millie. We still have a few things to get ready before tomorrow." Hazel arched her brows and nodded toward the exit.

"We just got here," Millie complained.

Hazel tugged at her sister's arm rather roughly. "Millie...I'm tired. And these young people don't need us hanging over them, either. Now come on."

"Oh, all right." She pulled one of her exaggerated frowns, then smiled broadly at Kevin and Michelle. "See you two lovebirds in the morning." She blew them a kiss and let herself be dragged away. "What a simply wonderful Thanksgiving this is going to be," she said to her annoyed sister as they left the room.

"Simply wonderful," Michelle complained into the pillow, wincing at another back pain.

Kevin slapped his knees and stood. "Well, on that happy note, I think I'll call it a night, too." He bussed her forehead and quickly stepped back, acting as if he'd just kissed a cobra and expected a strike. From a safe distance he said, "As soon as everyone's here in the morning and ready to go, I told the chaplain I'd call his office, then he'll come up and we'll get started."

Now she felt guilty. Why would he want to marry someone so moody? She caught her bottom lip between her teeth and stared at him through glassy eyes. She wanted to say she was sorry. Instead she said, "I love you, handsome."

A smile relaxed a few lines she hadn't noticed before. "And I love you, too, beautiful." Pushing off the doorjamb, he left in a flurry.

"Beautiful," she mumbled under her breath. "Right."

# Seventeen

---

Another sleepless night and Michelle felt worse than ever. The large, pungent floral arrangements balanced atop white pedestal bases on either side of the bed made her nauseous.

Millie fussed with her bed jacket while Hazel affixed a small, puffy veil to her freshly blow-dried hair. With Dr. Wilson's blessing, the head of the bed had been raised to a forty-five-degree angle, which Michelle had mistakenly assumed would ease her backache. If anything, the pain seemed worse.

Kevin had barely spoken to her all morning, choosing to pace the hall outside the room until the women were ready.

Millie leaned close to Michelle's ear and whispered, "You're strung tighter than a fiddle, dear. You must know Kevin's quite the catch. There's no mistake being made here today," she said more firmly. "Can't we see a little smile? Hazel brought a camera, and we want your babies to see how happy their mama and daddy were on their wedding day, don't we?"

"I'm sorry. You're right," Michelle said, patting Millie's shaking hand. "Thank you for all you've done ... and for being here with me." She reached out for Hazel's hand and gave it a gentle squeeze.

"We've loved every minute of this week, Michelle," Hazel said. "Now, let's see." She rubbed her hands together, her eyes dancing with excitement. "You have something new—your jacket and veil. We need something old, something borrowed and something blue."

Michelle held up her white gold chain with the aquamarine pendant. "Here's something blue."

"Okay." Hazel reached into her breast pocket. "And here's something old and borrowed." She tucked her lacy hanky up the sleeve of Michelle's jacket, then stepped back and poised her camera in front of her face. "Let's get a couple of before pictures. Move in closer, sis."

The shutter clicked, and then Millie said, "Now you, Hazel," and took the camera.

Michelle noticed their matching rust-colored suits for the first time. Small feather-covered hats reminded her of early school days when she'd colored pictures of turkeys, which brought a smile to her lips.

After another click, Michelle said, "I think we're ready now." Her back was killing her. "If Paul's here, tell Kevin to get the chaplain up here so we can get this show on the road."

The sisters tried to beat each other to the door, their arms waving about with unbridled enthusiasm, keeping the smile on Michelle's face a little longer.

Paul walked in with Dr. Wilson and both men stopped short, taking in Michelle's bridal attire and the transformed room before nodding their approval.

Paul sauntered to Michelle's bedside, looking far more relaxed than she felt. He kissed her cheek, then rested his hand on her arm. "Kevin's a lucky man." His smile was warm and genuine. Then, turning sideways to include her OB, Paul said, "I hope you don't mind that I asked Larry to join us. I caught him coming out of Delivery."

Michelle pulled herself a little higher in the bed, trying to find a comfortable position, but she didn't succeed. "Glad you're here, Dr. Wilson," she said, reaching out her hand to shake his, which seemed a strange formality, considering the nature of their previous contacts. The thought occurred to her before that if he ran into her on the street he might not remember her face. Now maybe he would. She started to chuckle, then winced and let out a moan.

"Problem?" Dr. Wilson asked, back to playing his familiar role.

"Lots of back pain, all night and this morning. Probably tension thinking about wedding details."

His hands probed her belly through the sheet. With a practiced calm voice, he asked, "These pains—are they constant or do they come and go?"

"Come and go. More come than go this morning," she said, growing more anxious by the minute, seeing something in his demeanor that set off warning bells.

"Some women have contractions in the back, you know."

No. She didn't know.

"How often has this been happening? How close together?"

She hadn't been paying attention. She thought a moment, then let out a loader moan that brought her head up off the mattress. This one hurt far worse than the last.

"I guess that answers my question."

At that point a nervous Kevin raced into the room. Paul, the sisters and Reverend Potter strolled in behind him, chatting amicably, getting acquainted.

The chaplain moved directly to Michelle's side, a tattered black book clutched in his hands. "Are we ready to begin?" he asked.

Dr. Wilson turned and took them all in with a single glance. "I think Michelle has started without you."

It took a second, but then all at once everyone sucked in a loud gasp.

Kevin was first to speak. "You don't mean—"

The doctor held out his arms, herding the group back toward the door. "If everyone would wait outside a moment, I'll check and see."

Michelle caught Kevin's gaze and held it. The sudden panic she felt was mirrored on his face. "Can Kevin stay?" she asked the doctor, her eyes still on Kevin.

"If you'd like," he said, closing the door behind the others. Moving quickly, he pulled on a latex glove, pulled back the sheet and bent her knees. Unlike the past, when he examined her this time, scorching pain shot through her entire body. She grabbed the side bars of the bed and gritted her teeth. Fortunately, he finished as quickly as he'd begun, and the pain started to subside. He covered her and patted her knee.

"If you two plan to marry this morning, you'd better hurry up. These babies have plans of their own."

Kevin moved closer to Michelle, taking her damp hand in his own sweaty palm. "How far is she dilated?" he asked.

"Over four. And it's my guess she's moving rapidly."

Kevin gazed down at Michelle's flushed face. "We should wait till later, don't you think?"

She could no longer see him clearly—her vision was blurred from pain and the tears that brimmed at her lashes—but she held firm to his hand. "No, Kevin. I know it sounds silly, old-fashioned ... but I want us to be married *before* the babies are born. Don't you?"

"Yes, of course." He dabbed a tissue under her eyes, removing the mascara that had begun to smear. "It's your call, sweetheart. We can start, but anytime you want to stop, you know I'll understand."

She started to cry in earnest now. "I've been so rotten to you lately. I'm sorry, Kevin."

"Shhh ... It's okay."

"Owww ..." she howled, grabbing her belly.

Dr. Wilson moved to the door. "If you're determined to do this, Michelle, we have to get moving. Should I let the others in?"

She hadn't planned to sell tickets to this event, but what choice did she have? They needed witnesses and a chaplain. "Yes, yes. Let's hurry."

Dr. Wilson took charge, positioning everyone for maximum privacy. The chaplain stood close to Kevin with his back to Michelle's bent knees. Millie, Hazel and Paul took similar places on the opposite side. All but Paul looked ill. He seemed calm, smiling. He motioned a passing nurse into the room and then gave Kevin a knowing look.

Michelle wondered what that was all about, but quickly forgot the question when another contraction hit full force.

Wilson spoke to the nurse. "Notify Neonatal. Get me more help, and an isolette. We might be delivering here." He pulled the sheet out from the foot of the bed and folded it back just below Michelle's knees, leaving her some measure of modesty.

The minister began, "Dearly beloved, we have gathered here today..."

Wilson inserted what felt like an entire gloved hand and Michelle bucked off the mattress. "Ahhh!"

"She's already at six. Can we skip ahead?" Wilson asked curtly.

The minister flipped the pages and obliged nervously, ad-libbing the first part. "Do any of you know a reason we shouldn't continue? Legally or otherwise?" All heads shook and he hurried on. "Please join right hands." He looked up and saw they already had. "Do you, Kevin, take this woman, Michelle, to be your wife, promising to love her, honor her, cherish her and keep her so long as you both shall live?"

"Whoo, whoo, whoo, whoo. Oh, God. *Kevin!*" Michelle shouted his name and he stooped down beside her.

"Focus, sweetheart. Look at my eyes and nowhere else."

She did as he said, sweat running into her eyes, making her blink rapidly. "Whoo, whoo, whoo." She started to cry. "Kevin, this isn't working. It hurts."

"Do you want to stop?"

"*Yes!* Let me out of here." She started to sit up. "I want to go home."

Kevin pushed her back gently. "The ceremony... Should we stop the wedding?"

The pain gradually faded to tolerable. "No. Just hurry. Please."

Kevin turned back to the chaplain who repeated, "Do you?"

"Do I what—? Oh! Yes, yes. I do."

Millie and Hazel sniffled, and the sound of the camera shutter was lost in the chaos.

"Whoo, whoo, whoo..." Michelle tried again, mascara now trailing down her hot cheeks. "Owww...whoo, whoo, whoo..." She glared at Kevin who just stood there. Pain-free. "Whoo,

whoo, whoo..." She raised up on her elbows and shouted at him. "Whose idea was this Lamaze thing, anyway? Drugs...I need drugs... Whoo, whoo, whoo... Ahhhhhh..."

She lay back and turned her wrath on the minister. "Hurry up. Ask me before another one comes," she said, mincing no words.

"Do you, Michelle, take this man, Kevin, to be your husband, promising to love him, honor him, cherish him and keep him so long as you both shall live?"

She was thinking, *At this rate that won't be long.* A piercing pain exploded near her cervix and she screamed. Now she lay in a river, the pain constant, more intense.

Wilson said, rather matter-of-factly, "Her membrane ruptured."

"Oh, God! Am I going to die?" She stared deep into Kevin's eyes, searching for the truth, finding only a glimmer of a smile.

"Your water broke, sweetheart."

"Then why in the hell didn't he say so instead of scaring me half to death?"

The doctor ignored her complaint, driving her panic to the edge. Oh, God. They didn't know it, but she *was* going to die. Of that she was certain. The pain had doubled, tripled, gone off the scale. Bad menstrual cramps. Bull. That was like issuing small-craft warnings for a hurricane.

Suddenly she had to push. But how? How was she going to get these two basketballs through that meager passage? It wasn't anatomically possible.

"Hee, hee, hee..."

"I can see the head, Michelle," the doctor announced calmly.

"Hee, hee, hee..."

The chaplain leaned forward. "You didn't answer the question, Michelle."

"*What question?*" she shouted in his face. He jumped back, assuming correctly that she wanted to strangle him.

Another man. Another pain-free, useless male.

"Do you take Kevin..."

She felt her face grow scarlet as she hunched forward and pushed with all her might. With a rather unladylike grunt, she finally said, "Yes, yes. I do."

"By the power invested in me by God and the state of Michigan..."

"Hee, hee, hee..."

"One more push, Michelle. You're almost there."

"...I now pronounce you husband and wife."

Red-faced, Michelle hunched forward again, Kevin's one arm bracketed around her shoulders, the other under her arm. She pushed down on him, and he held her tight. "Uhhhhhggggg."

She felt instant relief at the same moment she heard the tiny wail. She slumped against Kevin and peered around her knees.

"This one's a girl," the doctor said, smiling warmly at Michelle. Then he looked at Kevin. "Want to cut the cord, Dad?"

Dad. Happy tears stung Michelle's eyes. She watched as Kevin—her husband—slipped on a glove with professional ease and then snipped the cord.

Paul was right beside him, a syringe full of blood in one hand, a basin for the cord in the other. He gave both to a nurse and shouted, "Stat!" as the young woman rounded the corner.

Michelle didn't have time to question what that was about, because it all began again.

"You may kiss the bride," the chaplain said in a quiet voice, sounding as if he'd rather be anywhere else.

"Later, Padre. Hee, hee, hee..." Thank you, God, she prayed silently, for a healthy little girl. "Hee, hee, hee..." And for not giving me triplets.

Somewhere in the distance she heard a loud thud, but she was too busy to look. Another nurse scurried past the end of the bed and Kevin returned to her side. For some reason, she was less angry with him now, and she welcomed his strong arms.

Soon it would be over. "Hee, hee, hee..."

"Push, Michelle," the doctor repeated.

But not soon enough, she discovered as she fell back and waited for the next one. Kevin brushed her wet hair off her forehead and she smiled up at him. "We have a little girl."

"You're beautiful, Mrs. Singleton. I love you."

"I love you . . . hee, hee, hee . . . too."

"You're crowning, Michelle. Push harder," the doctor instructed.

She pushed as hard as she could, bearing down on Kevin's willing arm, but no baby's cry rewarded her efforts. She fell back against the pillow again, not knowing where the strength would come from if this lasted much longer.

A nurse came running into the room as if she'd been shot from a cannon and Paul grabbed a paper from her hands. He read it quickly, then handed it to Kevin.

Kevin read the words in front of him, then bowed his head. Frightened, Michelle gripped his arm. "Is something wrong? Is our little girl okay?" Panic rose up and lodged in her throat as another contraction brought her upright. "Hee, hee, hee . . ." In spite of the pain, she couldn't take her eyes off Kevin's bent head. Finally he looked up, gazing deep into her eyes, tears streaming down his handsome face.

"The blood type is AB negative, Michelle."

"I think this one will do it," the doctor said, interrupting. "Push hard."

With every ounce of her reserves, she pushed and growled with determination. And as before, she heard a healthy cry and fell back against the pillow, thankful the worst was over.

"And this little guy completes the set." Dr. Wilson held him high enough for Mama to see without moving.

Again Kevin cut the cord, returning quickly to Michelle's side. "I'm so proud of you. You did it, sweetheart."

A nurse leaned in the doorway. "Did someone order an epidural?"

Dr. Wilson nudged her out ahead of him. "Congratulations, you two. I'll be back after I check on the babies."

Drugs! Where were they when she needed them? But now that it was over, she was glad it had worked the way it did. Her babies were healthy. Correction—*their* babies.

Her eyes widened. Wait a minute. What had Kevin said just before . . .

"Kevin! Did you say AB negative?"

He nodded, smiling down at her through shining eyes.

"Then that means—"

"I'm the father. The natural, biological father. So what do you say to that, Mrs. Singleton?"

"I say *great!* Maybe two is enough." She laughed, not certain she'd feel that way tomorrow. But for now, she couldn't imagine needing or wanting anything else. She had a wonderful husband, two perfect babies and dear, dear friends.

She heard the click of the shutter this time and looked in the direction of the camera.

"Oh, Millie! I look terrible," she said, patting the headpiece that clung stubbornly to a knot of her wet, tangled curls.

"No, you don't. The two of you look wonderful, happier than I've ever seen anyone, anywhere." She clicked again and Michelle gave up, laughing softly against Kevin's sturdy shoulder.

"Where's Hazel?"

"She's resting in another room for a while. She got a little bump on her head when she hit the floor, but she's okay." She waved her hand, urging them not to worry. "I always was the hardier one in the family." She chuckled as she kissed Michelle's forehead.

"You're a very brave young woman, my dear. I never could have done what you just did."

"Me either," Paul said as he reentered the room. He clasped the foot of the bed and smiled at the trio. "I just came from NICU. The babies weighed in at four pounds, six ounces, and four-eight. The boy's the bigger one. They'll incubate them overnight, but barring any unforeseen event, Wilson said to tell you two things—as soon as you're able to get yourself down there, you can hold them, and you may even be able to take them home with you when you leave."

"Oh, Paul," Michelle said, swallowing another lump in her throat. "Thank you for that . . . and for everything."

She heard the legs of a chair scrape against tile somewhere in the vicinity of a floral arrangement. Reverend Potter shuffled to the side of her bed a moment later, looking as if he'd just returned from an all-night binge.

"I'm sorry, Reverend," Michelle said sheepishly. "I wasn't very kind to you earlier. . . ."

Wearily he held up a hand. "That's quite understandable. But now can we finish the ceremony?"

Kevin swiveled around and peered up at him. "I thought we did."

"Didn't someone tell me there were rings?"

Simultaneously Paul and Millie dug through their pockets until they found the gold pieces. They handed them to Kevin and Michelle, both laughing at their own oversight.

"Repeat after me," the chaplain began, then eyed the newlyweds. "You can do this at the same time if you wish." Michelle and Kevin nodded. "With this ring, I thee wed."

In unison, slipping the gold bands on each other's third finger, they said, "With this ring, I thee wed."

"Good. Now kiss the bride and sign this form," Reverend Potter ordered with a weak smile, "so I can get out of here."

The couple laughed and obliged him, the camera clicking twice more.

As soon as the minister left the room, Millie walked around the bed to Kevin and said, "As a witness to this event, I feel a certain responsibility to watch over this marriage. I expect you'll treat your wife like a queen, young man, or you'll have me to answer to." She waved a pointed little finger at him, then stood on tiptoe and kissed his cheek. "Remember this special Thanksgiving, children. Love each other always as you do today." She turned and waddled out, Paul taking her elbow for support and waving his farewell without looking back.

Michelle sniffled and said on a sigh, "Alone at last."

Kevin sat on the edge of the bed and held her tight, stroking her arm, and another wave of love shimmered through her.

"We'd better enjoy this while we can," he said. "We won't be alone much anymore."

"We'll find time, my love, don't you worry." She started to chuckle over his shoulder and he pulled back.

"What?" he asked.

"It just keeps playing over and over in my head, like a broken record—*AB, AB, AB*."

"That's what we should name them—*A* and *B*," he teased, a grin tugging at one corner of his mouth.

*AB, AB, AB...* "I got it," she said, holding her belly as she laughed. "Abbie...as in Abigail. How do you like that one?"

Kevin stroked his chin and squinted his eyes. "It could work. And Abe... as in Abel or Abraham."

"Abbie and Abe. I like it." She smiled.

"Abe and Abbie," he said. "Abe's bigger."

"Abbie's older and most certainly wiser for many years."

"Maybe till high school, then watch out."

They eyed each other and the laughter subsided.

"May I kiss the bride again?" Kevin whispered softly, pulling her into his warm embrace.

"Again, and again, and again, my love."

Hazel leaned against her sister in the doorway as Millie finished the last of the film.

"They don't even know we're alive right now, do they, Millie?" Hazel asked with a wistful smile.

Millie pocketed the spent roll of film before taking her sister's elbow and tiptoeing away. "We done well on this pair, don't you think, sis?"

Hazel patted her sister's arm and sighed as they weaved their way down the bustling hospital corridor.

"Our best one ever, Millie. Our best one ever."

\* \* \* \* \*

Your very favorite Silhouette miniseries
characters now have a BRAND-NEW story in

### CHRISTMAS KISSES

Brought to you by:

## LINDA
# HOWARD

## DEBBIE
# MACOMBER

## LINDA
# TURNER

LINDA HOWARD celebrates the holidays with a **Mackenzie**
wedding—once Maris regains her memory, that is....

DEBBIE MACOMBER brings **Those Manning Men** and
**The Manning Sisters** home for a mistletoe marriage as
a single dad finally says "I do."

LINDA TURNER brings **The Wild West** alive as
Priscilla Rawlings ties the knot at the Double R Ranch.

Three BRAND-NEW holiday love stories...by romance fiction's
most beloved authors.

Available in November at your favorite retail outlet.

### ▼ Silhouette®
™

## MILLION DOLLAR SWEEPSTAKES
### AND EXTRA BONUS PRIZE DRAWING

## SILHOUETTE®

September's MAN OF THE MONTH title

**TALLCHIEF'S BRIDE**
Book 2 of

by bestselling author
**CAIT LONDON**

All Calum Tallchief wanted was a nice, traditional
wife and a couple of kids to fill his lonely home in
Amen Flats, Wyoming. But the least likely woman
to be his wife was somehow wearing the Tallchief
ring, sharing his bedroom, gossiping with his relatives
and dreaming of motherhood…all without any
intention of becoming his bride!

What is September's MAN OF THE MONTH to do?

Don't miss the sexy second book of **The Tallchiefs**
miniseries by Cait London, available in September,
only from Silhouette Desire.

# As seen on TV!
# *Free Gift Offer*

With a Free Gift proof-of-purchase from any Silhouette® book, you can receive a beautiful cubic zirconia pendant.

This gorgeous marquise-shaped stone is a genuine cubic zirconia—accented by an 18" gold tone necklace.

(Approximate retail value $19.95)

# Send for yours today...
## compliments of ▼ *Silhouette*®
TM

To receive your free gift, a cubic zirconia pendant, send us one original proof-of-purchase, photocopies not accepted, from the back of any Silhouette Romance™, Silhouette Desire®, Silhouette Special Edition®, Silhouette Intimate Moments® or Silhouette Yours Truly™ title available in August, September or October at your favorite retail outlet, together with the Free Gift Certificate, plus a check or money order for $1.65 u.s./$2.15 can. (do not send cash) to cover postage and handling, payable to Silhouette Free Gift Offer. We will send you the specified gift. Allow 6 to 8 weeks for delivery. Offer good until October 31, 1996 or while quantities last. Offer valid in the U.S. and Canada only.

## *Free Gift Certificate*

Name: _____

Address: _____

City: _____ State/Province: _____ Zip/Postal Code: _____

Mail this certificate, one proof-of-purchase and a check or money order for postage and handling to: SILHOUETTE FREE GIFT OFFER 1996. In the U.S.: 3010 Walden Avenue, P.O. Box 9077, Buffalo NY 14269-9077. In Canada: P.O. Box 613, Fort Erie, Ontario L2Z 5X3.

---

## FREE GIFT OFFER                                            084-KMD
ONE PROOF-OF-PURCHASE
To collect your fabulous FREE GIFT, a cubic zirconia pendant, you must include this original proof-of-purchase for each gift with the properly completed Free Gift Certificate.

---

**084-KMD**

The exciting new cross-line continuity series about love, marriage—and Daddy's unexpected need for a baby carriage!

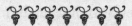

You loved

***THE BABY NOTION*** by Dixie Browning (Desire #1011 7/96)
and
***BABY IN A BASKET*** by Helen R. Myers
(Romance #1169 8/96)

Now the series continues with...

***MARRIED...WITH TWINS!*** by Jennifer Mikels
(Special Edition #1054 9/96)

The soon-to-be separated Kincaids just found out they're about to be parents. Will their newfound family grant them a second chance at marriage?

Don't miss the next books in this wonderful series:

***HOW TO HOOK A HUSBAND (AND A BABY)***
by Carolyn Zane (Yours Truly #29 10/96)

***DISCOVERED: DADDY***
by Marilyn Pappano (Intimate Moments #746 11/96)

DADDY KNOWS LAST continues each month...
only from

**▼** *Silhouette*®
™

Look us up on-line at: http://www.romance.net

DKL-SE

# You're About to Become a

## *Privileged Woman*

Reap the rewards of fabulous free gifts and benefits with proofs-of-purchase from Silhouette and Harlequin books

# Pages & Privileges™

It's our way of thanking you for buying our books at your favorite retail stores.

Harlequin and Silhouette—
the most privileged readers in the world!

For more information about Harlequin and Silhouette's PAGES & PRIVILEGES program call the Pages & Privileges Benefits Desk: 1-503-794-2499

Silhouette®

SD-PP172